My love for stories started wi[...] me to prepare one for our week[ly ...] ber being in the taxi on my way [to her flat, lost in my imagination,] peering up at the large Parisian maple trees that swooshed passed my window. She was a person that taught me to love without reserve, to offer your best smile to the world and, to pour your heart into everything you do, regardless of how vulnerable this made me. This way of loving has been the cement for the foundations of all the wonderful relationships I have today. Reaching out to everyone with a smile and including every soul as my friend, has also attracted great darkness and even death; despite this pain and loss, the relationships I have gained have grown to be my fuel. Passion is like a hydrocarbon, the more volatile and explosive, the brighter the light of its flame and, the greater the pain of its burn. Those that I love give me the faith, support and kindness that allow me to write, climb mountains and build businesses. I achieve my goals thanks to the constant embrace of all your arms around my neck, I carry them like medals, your love is both my support and my greatest achievement.

Chapter One

Riding Through Europe

All I wanted to do was to run away, but I would be shot if they caught me - these guys wouldn't ask questions.

It was ten of us, all crammed into this GAZ-33097 military transport vehicle. We were a long way from home, somewhere in Crimea, on our way to the front. It smelt of diesel and of men too far away from their wives.

We were the last ones of the convoy, with another twelve trucks advancing steadily ahead of us. I was sat on the edge of the bench; I felt so close to freedom I could nearly taste it. I knew I should jump - I might not get such a good opportunity for a while; I knew I was probably going to die anyway, but it just felt too soon.

I felt frustrated at the idea of dying without having achieved much. Besides, I had to tell someone about what my father had discovered, it would change everything; I couldn't die without passing it on. The truck took a right turn, lumbering onto a bridge. As we progressed, I looked at the sea below; from afar it looked inanimate and motionless, slowly fading away as we rose up the bridge's arc. If I jumped, this would be painful - more painful than a bullet in my head. While I toyed with this idea, a sudden, deafening bang went off. It felt like a needle piercing my eardrums combined with a boxing glove to my temple. The shock paralysed me; I found myself stuck to my seat, fear turning my flesh to stone.

Amid this agitated confusion, Bordov, our officer, was frantically shouting at us to jump out of the truck and take our positions. I did so without thinking twice, landing heavily on the tarmac below. I could now see what had caused the explosion. A missile had hit the bridge ahead, blowing up the two trucks leading the convoy, which were now billowing plumes of black smoke. I looked around at my platoon: all were looking towards the explosion, hypnotised by the mangled charred bodies falling out of the flames. Maybe it was instinct, but I decided to gently put down my AK-12 on the ground and jump off the bridge, without even looking at the sea below.

The drop felt endless - time froze, adopting a different dimension, until I smashed hard against the water. After such a violent landing, I plunged into the darkness for what felt like an eternity; while underwater, a piercing pain flooded from my feet all the way up to my head. It reassured me; I was alive.

It felt quiet down there; a sense of peace enveloped my battered limbs. As I slowly floated back up to the surface, I was struck by a sudden fear - this is when they would start shooting at me. I knew I was not dead yet I felt somewhat detached, as if I had left my body and was observing the scene from a distance. As I approached my death, I thanked my Dad, feeling his smile fall tenderly upon me.

As my head jolted out of the water, I breathed hard, trying to gasp as much air into my lungs as possible. After a couple of seconds, I realised I hadn't been shot or even shot at, so I turned around and decided to face my executioners. To my surprise and relief, the current had brought me well out of shooting range, and the dots moving around on the bridge seemed to show no signs of having even seen me. I floated on my back downstream, ditching my belt and load-bearing vest, which was empty as we had been told we would get ammunition at the front.

The water was hostile, a glacial blanket wrapping my body tightly. The cold was helping soothe the pain in my legs, but was also starting to get to me; I could survive but it had become a race against time. I had to get out of there one way or another. It was November and the sea was starting to get bitterly cold. I later found out that I had jumped off a bridge just past a town called Mayaki, surrounded by Lower Dniester National Park, which was a couple of kilometres from Moldova.

When I eventually got to shore, I ran to take cover by some trees, took my drenched clothes off, and tried to get as much water out of them by twisting them, as we had been taught in our very rudimentary training. As I put my cold soggy clothes back on, I started shivering. My breathing had become an uncontrollable series of hiccups; somehow the pain had left, giving place to a deep chill that I felt go down to the marrow of my bones. I started to run as best as I could. My knees felt rusty, and my shoulders heavy. After a few kilometres, my body started to return to a normal temperature, and the pain settled back in, but I knew that as soon as I stopped, I would return to a hypothermic state.

That's when I spotted the boat - it was black and no bigger than fifteen metres long. It was as still as a lily floating peacefully on a pond. As I had been running for a while and hadn't come across anything else, I decided that this may be my last chance to beg for, and hopefully secure some warmth; it would be my ticket to freedom.

I approached the boat with feline alertness to any noise or movement. I observed the vessel for a while, looking for movement through the few widows it had, but everything was still. On my guard, I gently walked down the pier and stepped onto the deck. My heart was pumping hard against my chest, my mouth was dry, and fresh adrenaline was shooting through my veins to dope my muscles. My every movement was sharpened by fear. I looked through the small porthole in the door. No one seemed to be inside; I hesitantly turned the doorknob and slipped into the dimly lit room. I was taken aback by its almost unnatural tidiness, which felt unusual for what looked like a fishing boat: there was barely anything in the room other than a map on the table, which was set in the centre with a pair of rather expensive looking binoculars left on the boat's dashboard. The instrument panel was covered in a variety of lights, dials, and switches. I knew nothing about boats, but this clearly wasn't your regular local fishing boat. Why the hell would there be a fishing boat in the middle of a zone of conflict? As that thought paved its way through my mind, I saw someone; a man, with a shaved head, dressed in a heavy dark blue overall, smoking a cigarette that seemed to be coming to its end. Not thinking twice, I ducked behind the dashboard. My eyes darted around the small room, desperate to find a place to hide. I saw a door that led to a short flight of steps followed by a corridor - it was the only door other than the one I had just come through, I had no choice, so swiftly crept down the stairs, closing the door behind me. It was warm down here and there was a strong smell of gasoline that reminded me of the truck I had just been in. The dimly lit corridor, which was no more than five metres long, had two doors on each side and one at the end. As I stood there for a second trying to decide which one to open, the door in the room above slammed shut; whoever that man was, he had finished his cigarette and was now getting dangerously close. If he came down to the underdeck, I was done. I decided I would go for the door at the end of the corridor, somehow feeling that the further away from the man above, the better. I was relieved when I carefully twisted the knob and it swung open, the darkness behind the door was reassuring. The faint light of the corridor trickled down another short flight of steps. I couldn't see much but instinctively knew it must be the hull of the boat. I stepped down, closing the door behind me. Suddenly I was plunged into complete darkness, I stood there for a moment not knowing what to do next. I felt oddly reassured by the light deprivation, the humid warmth, and the sudden stillness of the place. I decided to palpate the area around the door until I came across the light switch. As the neon lights flickered on, dazzling me with their heartless whiteness, I scanned the room. Ahead of me was a tube-like staircase, which led down to the centre of a triangular room - I was clearly at the bow of the boat. Other than a large rope in a curated pile, a pile of empty jerry cans, and a large folded dark green canvas behind the stairs, the room was bare. I felt this was good news as no one would need to come down here. I froze for a few seconds, holding my breath to focus on the noises above me. The thud of footsteps felt very distant, almost imperceivable - they wouldn't hear me down here. So I decided to carefully arrange the jerry cans in a line, piling the canvas on top, and unfolding it a little so that I could use it to cover myself. When I felt satisfied with my work, I went to switch off the lights, fumbling back to my dark little nest.

Time and space took a new course. I waited under my newly created bubble of canvas warmth. It reminded me of my childhood, jumping into my cold bed and pulling the duvet over my head, breathing out of my mouth like a goldfish. A calmness enveloped me and my muscles released their tension. I waited, listening for noises. I could hear distant voices, they were like flickering stars in the darkness of the night. The cigarette man wasn't the only one on board, he was having a discussion with someone, I concentrated hard to make out the words, but couldn't even recognise the language they were speaking. My mind started to wonder whether it would be better to be caught down here by Ukrainians or Russians. These thoughts were interrupted by a terrible rumbling. The engines had been started. All other noises were drowned out, the stars died out and only darkness remained, off I went towards an unknown destination. Powerless to the direction the boat was taking - but feeling good about being abandoned to my fate. Gently rocked by the sea, in my cradle of jerry cans and canvas, I fell into a deep sleep.

The absolute and uninterrupted darkness led me to a strange place; one in which I couldn't make out whether I was sleeping or awake. When I opened my eyes it was dark, when I closed them flashes of memories would flash by. I must have been in and out of sleep as I kept on waking up feeling very thirsty, my mouth was so dry I couldn't even muster enough saliva to clean it. Again and again, I rubbed my tongue on my palate, shovelling thick paste towards the back of my throat. Trying to go back to the painfulness of sleep. As time passed, punctuated by nothing but darkness, my throat started to feel like it had swallowed a bunch of razor blades, which were slowly making their way down it. I was so thirsty and my bladder was about to burst. I found a jerry can that didn't smell of petrol and popped my penis in it, relieving my bladder with an endless trickle. I then drank the content with big gulps, surprised at how nice drinking my own pee was. I think I smiled, sitting there on my island of darkness - I had sorted out both my bladder and throat problems - it made me feel proud. The satisfaction dipped me back into a slumber - maybe it was asleep - maybe I was just drunk with fatigue. The depths of darkness wrapped their thick blankets around me, hundreds of layers, holding me down, till they erased my existence.

The pain in my throat came back and was now combined with a deep hunger eating away at my stomach. Either the pain or the darkness was getting to me as even when I had my eyes open, any lack of focus would lead me to hallucinate. I kept on seeing my father, he sat next to me and was repeatedly telling me to find a person to pass on the secret, like a scratched record. I told him to stop it, aware that I was going crazy - I knew I couldn't last much longer down here and started to consider putting an end to it, but going up and handing myself in. For how long this thought swayed in and out of my mind I have no idea, I would push it away and it would come back, each time it was stronger and more convincing, each time I was weaker and closer to breaking. Time and I were both lost in this same darkness fighting against each other. I jumped out of the endless slumber when the boat's horn went off, like electrocuted, I was back to full alert. The boat was reaching its destination, and while I had no idea where this could be, a huge feeling of relief paved its way through my entire body - I stretched my legs out in the darkness, getting ready to move after what felt like an eternity of stainless. A shadow of doubt then started to make its way from my head to my chest, my breathing became constricted by anxiety. I was thinking about how the hell I was going to get out of this bloody boat, I had no clue who was even driving it, but was pretty convinced that considering the green canvas, the high-tech dashboard and the blue cigarette man, it wasn't a bunch of fishermen. For all I knew, I was on a Russian boat heading to get court-martialed. I thought of running up the stairs and jumping off the deck, taking the men by surprise and hoping they didn't have any loaded guns handy. Mulling this over a few times I concluded that if they were going into port, there would be no more cigarette smoking, and no distractions - this was a plan B and not a plan A. I then remembered there had been a porthole on the side of the boat's hull - I concluded that if there wasn't one in the room I was in it was most likely behind one of the two doors on either side of the corridor I had passed. The sailors would likely be in the control cabin or on the deck while entering the port, so the coast would be clear. In any case, it was a lot better than the other option. I creeped out from under the canvas, as carefully as a blind man can, crawling around and palpating the ground around me until I managed to get up the stairs. I paused to listen for any movement, my heart was beating so, the engines were still blearing, drowning any hope of hearing the men above - time was running out. I mustered up my courage, reached up and twisted the doorknob. Suddenly, a shaft of dazzling light shot out of the door opening, stabbing my blinded eyes. I closed the door, returning to being blinded by darkness rather than light. I decided to switch the lights on and adapt before heading out. The change of light was so aggressive that my eyes remained firmly closed for a while - the only way to open them was to do so gradually, with my hands cupping them - letting the light filter through inch by inch. It was a slow process and I knew time was running out. As I faced the door again, my heart got to work again, and the arteries in my neck swelled - getting me ready to run. I opened the door onto the empty corridor and without much more thought, I darted to the left door. Thankfully it was unlocked and swung open - I had given up on caution at this point.

I suddenly found myself in an empty small bedroom, painted white, with two bunks to one side and a little desk on the other. In the middle was the porthole, which looked a lot smaller in reality than in my imagination. It didn't look like it was going to be an easy squeeze. I lifted the latch, poed it open and popped my head straight through it, wiggling my shoulders, slowly and painfully till they got through. I managed to pass my right arm but the left one remained stuck and it seemed that the more I shuffled to free it, the harder it got to move it. That's when I heard a voice behind, muttering "what the fuck.." A sudden bolt of fear struck through my body, propulsing my hips out of the tight orifice - I flopped clumsily into the sea below, my body screaming at the violent slap of the freezing water. As I came back up, I saw a little head popping out of the porthole. He had short blonde hair which was blowing against the wind, he was looking at me with a mixture of confusion and astonishment drawn on his face. While I swam back towards the shore, I realised he had spoken English. I kept on swinging my head to look at the boat which was getting smaller on the horizon, praying for it not to turn round. For some reason, it didn't.

Luckily the boat had been fairly close to the coast at the time, so I managed to make it to the beach alive. If it wasn't for the weight of my uniform and the severe lack of food and water, it might have even been a fairly easy swim. I sat on the beach, feeling very lightheaded, so drained that I couldn't even think of what to do next, I was scanning the landscape without even really processing or even seeing any of it. Although I was getting very cold and my brain was telling me to get moving, my body remained limp - it took a little while to muster the energy to stand up. By then my eyesight got back to normal, and I noticed a tiny woman walking towards me with her dog. Her grey hair was tied in a bun which sat on her tiny head like a wedding cake. Her face showed no emotion, neither surprise nor fear. Her wrinkles drew a deep and permanent frown on her face. I was tempted to go towards her and ask her for directions but she just kept on walking, straight past me, pretending not to notice me - it felt like we were separated by an entire world or dimension - for a second it made me think I might be dead.

The pain going through my entire body quickly made me realise this wasn't the case, and that a wet man, randomly appearing on a beach in military uniform was a style I needed to trade. Turning around, I saw the woman walking away in the distance, calling someone on her mobile phone. Whoever it was, authorities would be alerted, either by her or the people on the boat.

Back to running it was - although this time it started as more of a shuffle as I struggled to clamber up the hill. The scenery, the old woman and the boatman's accent made me think that I was likely in England. The green hills rolling gently towards the dim horizon, the cosy-looking villages of little white houses with the grey hues of their slate roofs matching the clouds above. How the boat got me from Crimea to England was inconceivable. I would have had to cross the entire Mediterranean. How much time did I spend in that hull? All I knew was that it felt like a long time and that my shuffle was getting slower - I started to feel really faint, collapsing a couple of times as I went down a hill towards the valley below. I eventually got to a stream and fell to my knees, dunking my head into the water and drinking long gulps of what felt like the best water I had ever tasted. It hurt a lot at first, it was as if my throat was sewn shut, but the thirst drew me into a trance. I lay on my belly, sticking my face further into the cold water. By the time I decided that any more water would make me throw up, I had decided that walking downstream wasn't a bad idea, my scent would be lost and if they were British, it was likely they would have dogs. I got to the middle of the strong stream and let myself be carried downstream by the current, crawling over stones and driftwood. The cold started to send shards down my bones so I crouched for a rest on the side of the stream and came face to face with a frog. Without thinking, I pounced on it and shoved it into my mouth. I slowly masticated it, with the bones crunching as they mixed with the slime of its flesh, it was disgusting, and I belched repetitively, but something hidden deep within me helped me to keep it in. I realised I was starving and it had turned me into a wild animal. How long had it been since my last meal? I needed to find some food but turning up at someone's house, looking like this would only lead to my arrest. I had to find a place to hide, steal some clothes, and then get some food. I noticed a tall wall which was a few metres from the bank of the stream, deciding that whatever was behind it, would likely keep me safe. I climbed up it, using a nearby tree to lift myself up with the last of my energy. I rolled over it, falling into some thick bushes. My body was anaesthetised by the cold, so although it took me a while to get myself back up, there was no pain. Looking around, I realised I had stumbled into a beautifully curated garden. I remember my mother, who was an English teacher at the local university in Arkhangelsk (one of the larger cities in the arctic circle), telling me about the British obsession with tending to a garden. I had always loved this about the British and maybe that in some way, it had pushed me to become a star student in English and later, in Botanics. I knew that I had also been desperate to make her proud and honour her memory - especially after she died when I was fifteen. There was a little shed which I decided I made my way to and hid in. It seemed to be colder there than outside, and I decided I had had my dose of darkness, so it didn't take me long to go back out, in search of a better solution, which is when I came across a large steel and glass structure, filled with plants. It was quite something, I had read about these structures called greenhouses but had never experienced one on such a scale. It wasn't even just steel and glass, there was a neoclassical portico, with four large corinthian columns below its pediment. To either side of the stone entrance, a white steel skeleton jutted out, wrapping the hundreds of little panes of glass into a glorious ensemble of gentle lines. It was very quiet and I couldn't see anyone, so I went straight through the large heavy glass doors. It was enveloped in the humid warmth as soon as I stepped inside. After strolling carefully down the densely planted alleys, I decided to hide under a table in the far corner which had piles of plastic flower pots and half-open compost bags. I slowly got to work arranging them in a similar fashion to the jerrycans, so that I was concealed behind a protective wall of discarded material and got myself as comfortable as possible.

The peace the environment inspired me with did not last and despite my fatigue, I struggled to sit still. Whether it was extreme hunger, the desire to explore this wonder of a greenhouse or the acute pain emerging from my stomach, from hunger or the half-digested frog I was unsure, but my restlessness continued to surge. I decided to leave my hiding place again, and with little hope went in search of food. As if by some divine miracle, there was an entire section with the most wonderful cherry tomatoes. Those that crossed my eyes swiftly disappeared into my mouth - each one like a shiny ball of kindness exploding its sweet flesh into my mouth.

I looked up at the sky through the panes of glass, thanking whoever sent me here, my atheism suddenly overcome by my desperate gratitude. I also realised the sun was at its zenith which led me to assume the boat must have arrived at port rather early that morning. That explained the isolated old woman on the beach, that kind always wakes up early I thought, unable to sleep, hunted by their spiteful loneliness. While I was daydreaming - and probably quite high from the sugar rush of those tomatoes, I heard some female voices coming closer, and I quickly returned to my hiding place. The voices became closer and clearer until they were combined with their associated footsteps, climbing up the steps of the greenhouse. Peering through my wall of flower pots, I saw the confirmation that I was in England. Two young women strolled towards me, their beautiful slender figures, hovering gently from cactus to flower like a pair of swans.

The blonde girl was shorter, with dark blue eyes, like two little sapphires giving a slight judgemental severity to her features. Her straight golden hair, cut short, kissed her slender shoulders. Her body seemed in perfect proportion, as if at peace with her smaller size. She was wearing quite a short tartan skirt, wrapped around thick black tights which were tucked into stereotypically British rubber boots. She was the living epitome of the naughty English schoolgirl.

The taller lady was impossibly more beautiful than her friend. Not in the classic sense though. Maybe I was still high, but I felt she had an aura that I was instantly mesmerised by and far superseded canons of beauty. Her dark brown hair cascaded down her long black velvet coat, which flowed down to kiss her ankles. She had a long elegant neck, a small delicate nose assorted with two light brown almond eyes. Her elongated features, punctuated by delicate curves, reminded me of Iberian art, it was as if she had been the one to inspire Picasso in his early years. Her elliptical eyes gave her a confident feline look, her pupils, animated by an acute intelligence. Then I noticed her fingers, they were adorable, unusually short and chubby, as if they belonged to a child, contrasting with her intimidating elegance and offering a sense of approachable kindness. The short and chubby extremities were like ten little maharajas, armed by an entire collection of gold rings set with multicoloured stones, they were thick and seemed ready for war. Somehow this combination of elegance, innocence and strength made me understand she was very special.

They came in chatting to each other, and I heard her say, "It's rather warm here, I think I'd better take my coat off". Her voice was like the one you would expect from a BBC Radio Broadcaster in 1950. Elegant, confident, imperturbable yet approachable. As she abandoned her long, perfectly cut velvet coat, she revealed a beautiful red dress, which came down to her knees, with buttons from top to bottom along the front. It made her look like one of those perfect American housewives in those old ads for refrigerators. Yet she looked nothing like one of them, she was beyond perfection, the dress was honoured by her body, and its warm colour cherished the unique combination of elegance and innocence - so much so that the fabric held her gently but tightly, revealing her figure without vulgarising it.

I was so enthralled by her beauty, the way her fine lips rose slightly to form an enigmatic smile, her chubby fingers stroking the flower petals, that I didn't notice that my hand was resting on a rotten piece of wood, holding two of the table feet together. As I was drawn towards her, my nose creeping to smell her, my eyes peering through the pots for a better look at her, I leaned onto it further, until it snapped, and I rolled out of my hiding place in an explosion of flower pots and compost. Both girls jumped out of the way, letting out a little screech. I found myself, stretched out on my back like a starfish staring up at the ocean surface, unable to move, looking straight up at them.

"And who might you be?" she asked when she had collected herself. So I answered, still spread out on my back "Nicolas Popov". Maybe because I instinctively felt that this position of inferiority made me less threatening, or maybe it was because her beauty froze me into submission. I flushed at this thought and added, while still lying on my back, "I'm so so sorry about this". She just stared down at me and said "What are you doing here? You do know this is private property". I scrambled to my feet, in my wrangled humid uniform, deciding quickly that there was no use lying to such a mythological-looking creature. So I blurted out in a single breath, "I am a Russian student, I was conscripted, sent to the front, I can't hurt a fly, so…so I escaped and found myself on a boat which led to a beach…close from here. I was starving and needed to hide" After a short breath, I added. "If you tell anyone, I'll be sent back, and I don't even want to imagine what they do to runaway soldiers". She paused, looking at my pathetic state and asked. "So what do you want me to do about it?". I looked deep into her eyes and saw a glimmer of fear that disappeared as quickly as it came. She had realised the weight of her question. An opportunity had resented itself to me and I needed to tread carefully. "I don't want to ask for too much, but I need to rest for a day before I move on, and find my way to a place where I can work and build something new. If you could spare some bread and a blanket that would be a lifesaver". She looked at her blonde friend, who was slightly shaking her head. But she turned around, handed me her hand and said; "My name is Lily, this is my cousin Lottie, we won't tell anyone about this. I'll try to get you some things from the house but you need to leave tomorrow." I shook her beautiful hand, sighing in relief. She turned around and they both walked out, not giving me the time to thank her. I could hear them arguing in the distance. I fell to my knees, thanking my guardian angel.

She came back, alone this time and gave me a half loaf of bread, with a pot of mackerel paté and two bottles of water. She watched me in silence while I devoured the food. The flavours pricked my taste buds with vigour, food had never tasted so good. I thanked her profusely until she told me I was already starting to sound British. She asked me how I spoke such good English, so I told her about my mother. I also told her about my slightly weird obsession with Botanics and English history and Art. We talked about all sorts of things, from hallucinogenic cactuses to the fact I was just off Portsmouth, one of the largest British military ports. The boat I had hitched a lift with, was clearly on some special ops mission. Maybe it was because I hadn't spoken to anyone for so long, but it felt as if the seasons were changing as our conversation flowed like a tranquil but powerful mountain stream. It was natural, unawkward, transparent, and transported me away from my sad reality towards a more tranquil place of warmth and happiness. Our exchange must have lasted a while as it eventually started to get dark. She assured me that her cousin Lottie would keep our secret, pointed me to the closest tap where I could drink as I pleased, and told me to stay hidden as the gardeners were away for the weekend, but anyone from her family could walk in on me. She finished off by saying she would be back tomorrow. For the first time in a while, I slept a deep, comforting sleep

- it felt like I had been saved and everything would be okay. When waking up at dawn, a surge of anxiety took hold of me as I remembered I needed to continue my journey. I needed to leave the comfort of this enchanting crystal palace. Waiting patiently for Lily to arrive, hoping she would have the generosity to offer some provisions for the journey ahead. I waited for what felt like an eternity.

When she eventually did arrive, the sun was already high in the sky. She came in with a backpack and a paper bag. She walked in with a welcoming, confident and even challenging smile, asking me how I slept. She started to unpack the treasures she brought me, starting with a pot of Jam, a full loaf of bread, slices of ham in their plastic packaging, a wonderful bottle of beer and a full change of clothes. The idea of a beer felt like an inconceivable luxury to me, I couldn't even remember the last time I had had one. It felt like a scene in Mary Poppins, or Christmas come early. "Thank you for the clothes, I will be sure to return them as soon as I can"; I mumbled, a little embarrassed at my state of depravity, knowing that it was a promise I was unlikely to honour. "Well, no offence, but I don't think you would get very far wearing camo. Police came this morning and asked if we had seen someone dressed in military uniform. Naturally, I said no and asked my father, who of course hasn't seen you. I would be careful though as they are clearly on the lookout, someone must have seen you yesterday". That old bitch on the beach I thought - I knew it!. "Well I really don't know how to thank you, and hope that life will allow me to do so, sometime when I'm back on my feet". She looked at me, tenderly and said: "Look, Nicolas, there is no point in thanking me. To be honest, you look just like my twin brother, who died when I was 21. I don't know why, but it feels like you have been sent here to me, to help me figure something out, I just don't know what. It's the same feeling I have when I stare at the sea after a big storm, the large waves crashing towards me, the white foams expressing their excitement. That feeling that something is written in the constantly flowing energy of the swell - that I can't quite read - a truth I can only feel is right without being able to understand it as if it was a foreign language. All that I do know is that after speaking to you yesterday, I felt liberated like I had spent the afternoon with him. He was just like you, smart, so cultured and knowledgeable, around 6 foot 4, which must be around your height I imagine, other than the fact he had long hair, you have the exact same kind and confident expression. I don't know why I'm telling you this...but I cried when I left you yesterday, I think it was because I felt I had just been with Arthur, that was his name...I really felt he was alive, only to realise that it was you of course. But they were happy tears. Happy in the sense that I found him in you. But I also know that of course, you need to leave, so I'm destined to lose you, as if for the second time, sorry, I'm babbling." I looked into her eyes, they were unfocused and a little humid, she had left for a few seconds, lost in her memories. Her mouth abiding to the dictatorship of her innermost thoughts. I got closer to her and put her childlike hand between my large paws. I couldn't find anything to say, but the silence and the hands pushed me to stupidly blurt out: "I'm so sorry to hear about your loss". She looked at me and pressed my hand, and then slipped hers away. "I'm sorry, I don't know what got into me, anyway, all that to say that's it's not in my nature to help strangers, I don't think I have ever even given a penny to a beggar". She looked a little distressed, I smiled at her, telling her I found it quite funny she felt the need to apologise for her generosity. It was as British as it gets. She laughed. We then got onto lighter subjects. This time talking about ancient British history, I was fascinated by Bath which was one of the main ancient Roman settlements, its hot springs cleaning their legions. She had been to University there, studying politics. This led to a long discussion about the war in Ukraine, Putin and the current geopolitical situation. She was surprised at how well-informed I was, as she had assumed we had all been indoctrinated with Putinist propaganda. I had to explain that we still lived in a free country and that many of us read foreign press. She eventually said, changing the subject "Maybe I was a little cold when we first met. I just wanted to say, if you *need* to stay longer...". She then looked away from me, somewhere beyond the cactuses and added: "I don't think it's wise for you to go out there quite yet, it's probably best you stay low for another day or two." She then looked straight back into my eyes. It took me a lot of effort to hold her powerful gaze, I could see she was also forcing herself not to look away. It was like trying to force two magnets with opposite poles together. "I just don't think you need to be in a hurry, I mean." I told her that other than feeling I was overstaying her welcome, I was very comfortable in my new crystal palace (as I now referred to it to her great pleasure) and that I was by no means in a hurry. She gave me a long hug and left, without saying anything. I sat there, on the floor, my heart pounding, my head in the clouds, sweat pouring out of my armpits, and blood pumping into my penis as it started to cry for attention. My body had never reacted like this after a single hug. She was so different to the girls I had known at Uni, I felt I could tell her everything. That we had known each other for a long time even though I knew it had only been two days. That's when the thought of passing on my secret to her came to my mind. As soon as it did, the thought cemented itself and became a certainty. I was going to tell her that we were all going to die. She would share the weight of the truth with me.

Chapter Two

How I Landed In Your Garden

She returned the next day, at around nine in the morning. She was more beautiful than ever. Wearing some flared jeans and a tight orange knitted top, she looked like a model out of the 70s. There was a part of me that was desperate for another hug or even just a stroke. All I got was a smile, It was however close to being too much for me to handle. I still managed to smile back with all my teeth, my mouth extending from one end to another. As soon as I did this, I blushed and struggled not to look like an embarrassed teenager. I had already decided I needed to tell her the whole story, from A-Z. So after exchanging a few platitudes, I told her, in a suddenly serious tone. "Lily, I can't quite explain why, maybe it's your generosity, maybe it's the sincerity with which you talked about your brother yesterday or, maybe it's just because you're a great listener, but I have rarely felt I can trust someone and yet, although I barely know you, I feel I can tell you anything". I straightened up. "Basically, I have this secret, a secret that I need to share, but I don't really know where to start. It's also not a nice secret, but it concerns you directly." She looked at me inquisitively, with a bit of a smile, not quite sure if to take me seriously. "Well go ahead, you look very serious and I'm on a long three-hour walk today so, I have all my time". I took a deep breath, and off I went.

"Well, I guess the best place to start is at the beginning, I think a bit of context will help. I was born and raised in Moscow, after which we all moved to Arkhangelsk. It's one of the last large cities on the arctic circle, way above St Petersburg and just on the frozen banks of the White Sea. We had to move due to my father's job. He is...or was a Physics Professor and researcher, specialising in studying and monitoring the earth's magnetic core. I was only seven when we moved. I think my mother was pretty devastated at the change of scenery, there were days in winter when the sun would barely appear. Anyway, she died of cancer when I was fifteen, as I told you before. It may have been the weather, the fact she didn't know many people up there, or her longing to return to England, you see, she studied at LSE for three years, in the 90s. That's where she met my father, who was on an exchange at UCLA at the time. I feel she always wanted to return to London. Her love for England is probably why she always spoke to me in English during my childhood. When she died, my father and I became very close. Her last few months were a true torture, we saw her turn from her energetic self into a grey skeleton-like figure. After she passed, my father worked very long hours, I think he was trying to escape it all, but he would always come back for dinner, even if he had to go straight back to the lab after, and we would speak English, I guess because it both made us feel closer to her. In the last three months though, he spent his life in the lab, like a workaholic. I don't even know when he slept. You see, he had come across something very unusual - noticing that the earth's magnetic core, which flows from the south pole to the north pole, going straight through the very conductive Iron core of the earth, was slowly shifting. They had been monitoring the changes for about twenty years - mainly calculating the movements of the north exit point of the electromagnetic field. It used to be just above Greenland, where it has historically always been located. We know it has been stable for the last 700,000 years. We also know the earth's magnetic field has flipped many times in the past, and it hasn't caused much of an issue. It just happens within a few minutes or even seconds and rather than the current going from South to North, as it does today. It flows from North to South. We have an accurate record of this as stones containing Iron, mainly found in lava, are all slightly magnetised. Just like the dial of a compass, the magnetization of the stone points in the direction of the current, so up north to Greenland. Through carbon dating, we have also been able to trace that the earth's electromagnetic field has flipped about one hundred times in the last twenty million years. So about, on average every five hundred thousand years. As said, we haven't experienced a flip for the last seven hundred years, so one may say it's overdue, but in reality, as my father told me, it's a random process, so it doesn't necessarily carry much meaning". I was slightly running out of breath so paused, making sure she was still paying attention. When I met her glowing eyes, I continued. "During the past electromagnetic reversals, other than maybe during the extinction of dinosaurs, and other mass extinctions, this hasn't really been an issue, due to the flip happening quite fast as it means our magnetic field is not disturbed. However, my father was monitoring the fact that what we are currently experiencing, is what they called a *slow reversal*. We have observed this in space, and it's thought to be the reason for Mars losing its atmosphere". Lily was looking intently into my eyes, she really was a good listener I thought. I went on. "So basically, the earth's electromagnetic current runs from south to north, coming out in 2002 more or less in the middle of Greenland, this current helps protect the earth from all sorts of things such as solar winds (which are particles released by the upper atmosphere of the sun, travelling at supersonic speeds, some of which are highly radioactive), this in turn, provides us with a stable and protected atmosphere, so all we see from these solar winds are in the form of northern lights. Hence why they are seen at the north pole. Anyway, I'm getting carried away. To go back to my father - his findings estimated that the magnetic field is not flipping but slowly shifting, and its northern pole is now just next to the city he was posted in, in Siberia. They have calculated that this slow shift from Greenland to Siberia, rather than a flip, means it's going to take approximately four thousand years for our electromagnetic field to restabilize, rather than the typical minutes or seconds. What my father told me is that whether it's four thousand or even twenty years, there is no way we or any other large mammal will survive the shift". Lily looked a little puzzled. She said, "So you're saying that the world is going to end? Sorry, but this sounds a little crazy, why would the loss of our electromagnetic field lead to us all dying anyway?". I pursed my lips, I was just repeating what my father had tried his best to explain, in the simplest of ways, but I clearly wasn't as convincing as my farther. "Well, our electromagnetic field protects us from Solar Winds, without that protection, our atmosphere would get burnt, that's what happened to Mars. Basically, when this happens, we won't be able to breathe and our bodies will get burnt by the sun's radiation. That's just one of the effects, The second point is that our tectonic plates which are floating on the iron core, are magnetised towards the current magnetic pole, if this pole stops drawing them together, there will be an astronomical amount of volcanic eruptions, as plates shift away from each other, each of which will release vast amounts of ash and CO_2 into our already weakened atmosphere, this alone would make our planet unlivable. You can imagine a giant Pompei". Again, I paused to catch my breath. "The third effect is that we would suddenly be bombarded by high energy particles which have come from solar radiation and have built up over millions of years. They are currently stuck in what we call the Van Allen radiation belt, thanks to our magnetic field, which traps these energetic particles again, protecting our atmosphere". There was silence. Lily looked a little shocked but didn't show signs of confusion. I guess I told her all this in quite a matter-of-fact way as if I was helping her with her homework. She tilted her head backwards, showing off her beautiful neck line, it then swung to one side and her gaze met mine. She asked; "So according to your father; when is this going to happen?" I inhaled slowly through my teeth and answered: "Ten years, and two months. At least that's when we will lose our magnetic field. My father said we won't last long after that, maybe a matter of weeks or months for those that are well-equipped, hiding in bunkers". Lily went quiet for a moment. Her eyes seemed to be searching for something behind my shoulders. "And how did they come to that figure?". "Well, the fact is the main current has been moving for the last ten years from Greenland to its current point in Siberia, at a very constant and predictable rate. They calculated with a good degree of certainty that it was going to get to Kazakhstan, which would mean that the flow would not be able to go in a single direction, it would disperse, and we would have a minimum of twelve poles being created at random on the planet's surface, which would reduce the magnetic field to a fraction of what it is today, not enough to maintain Van Allans Belt and tectonics plates in place anyway." She put her hand on my knee and told me. "So we are going to die in ten years..." she said, as the silence that followed this statement lingered, her grave expression gave way to a little smile, it was even slightly malevolent. She then said "Look Nicolas, I thank you for trusting me with this secret but it's just a bit much. I can't have someone coming into my life and just telling me I'm going to die, let alone a Russian deserter who studied languages at University. I imagine the last few weeks have been intense for you, and I think you need some rest". My eyes widened. Her words stabbed me in the stomach, it was as if a different person had pronounced those last words. I had given away my deepest secret and she had made it clear she didn't believe me. I wasn't angry at her though, she could hardly be blamed. For the first time, it occurred to me that I must sound like I was completely mad. Of course, she didn't believe me, no one would want to believe me.

People believe what they want to hear. But calling me a Russian deserter was a direct attack and by no means necessary. My shoulders dropped, my spine lost all strength, and defeat deflated me. She could clearly see she had hurt me but didn't seek to comfort me. She looked at me with more of a grimace than a smile, it came from a place of pity, I didn't want pity - I wanted to be understood. I stood up, took a breath and said "I know I must sound crazy, maybe I am, but I haven't finished". She tugged on my arm slightly so that I would sit back down, looking at me like you would a three legged dog, and said, "well, I'm still on my long walk so go ahead, I'm all ears". "Okay, I told you I got all this information from my father right? Well, I didn't give you the context". I felt uncomfortable standing up in front of her so I sat back down beside her. "It was the last dinner we shared together, and I have a horrible feeling that it will stay that way". She looked at me, curious to know the rest, I had managed to recapture her attention. "When he had talked me through all of this, just like I have to you, he ended by saying that he was going to notify a senior official in the Kremlin about these findings and their resulting effect. He reminded me that people may not want to hear this, and that if he wasn't back in the next three days, he wanted me to pass on this confidential information to someone else. He also added that I shouldn't come after him, and that should he disappear - I should share the information with people outside of Russia, or at least stay clear of Russian authorities. If he didn't come back, it was evidence that they wouldn't be receptive to such information. You can imagine how scared I felt. He was not a tactile man but he gave me a long, strong hug that night, before going out into the snow and back to the lab. That was the last time I saw him". "Do you know what happened to him?" she asked. "I have a good idea, as you know, having studied Russian politics, we have a way of keeping people's mouths shut. Different ways actually, but they all lead to that person disappearing". I tried my best to keep my eyes dry as I pronounced these last words. I didn't want to think about what they had done to him. Lily sensed my distress forcing its way through my ivory face. She looked shocked, a light shiver making its way down her spine and she quivered like a leaf in the wind. She recompose herself and said: "Wait so you mean they get rid of people like in the soviet days?" I answered in a shallow voice. "I didn't think so until now, I knew they assassinated people but they always have a cover up - he just never came back. Why would he just disappear? Anyway, he seemed to know it was coming". "I'm so sorry to hear this..." she said empathetically. "I don't think he was scared of death" I said, "or even maybe a part of him was happy to join my mother, he also knew he only had ten years to go...anyway he made me promise to pass this message. I didn't know who to, I haven't even had much time to think about it, but I chose you, or should I say, a series of events did, but it seems you don't believe me. Don't worry, I'll find someone else to pass it to." I suddenly realised how corny that last sentence sounded, it made my soul melt away. Luckily, she didn't seem to react, so much so that the silence got a little uncomfortable. She eventually said; "have some rest Nicolas, you're going to need it. My walk is coming to an end. We both stood up, she got close to me, so close I could smell her inebriating perfume, it was the smell of summer, with hints of lemons mixed with the musky smell of wood. She kissed me on the cheek, and left.

I spent the rest of the night up, I was in a swirl of contradicting emotions. I hated her for calling me a deserter and a madman, yet that kiss also stuck in my mind, I couldn't sleep and shifted restlessly on my compost bag mattress. What had been so comfortable a day ago now felt cold and unwelcoming. I started doubting my sanity, or maybe my father had lost it. I knew he had been pretty depressed since the death of my mother. Maybe he just went crazy, told me this story and went off to kill himself somewhere. I felt a pang of guilt - not believing I could even think such horrible thoughts. Thoughts can be so unforgiving, so far from what we actually believe, as if we are throwing a ball against a wall to see how it bounces back. No, my father had never diverged for the realms of sanity, he was sane, I knew this with my heart and my gut - he had a secret, and he was silenced.

Suddenly, a flash went through my mind, like a bright light. I remembered the fact that I had been conscripted to join the army just two days after my father's disappearance. At the time I had not made the connection, but maybe that was an effort to keep me under a close eye. If that was the case, my disappearance was going to attract the Kremlin's attention.

Chapter Three

At the Foot of the Mountain

I have to say that when Lily came the next morning, I may have been a little cold. I was angry at her. I woke up feeling humiliated. Not only did she not believe me, but she seemed to pity me like a begging madman on the side of the street. She had looked at me with pity in her eyes. Pity is the one thing I simply cannot stand. People gave me that look when my mother died. I mean, it's not because you go through hardship that you're suddenly some sort of weak, pathetic animal. She was clearly a very sensitive person as she could tell I was upset. She did her best not to let it affect her good mood. She was clearly excited about something. "I have great news Nick" she said in a cheerful tone. No one had ever called me that, other than my mother, I have to say - it instantly calmed me down. I asked her what it was, in a sheepish tone, I could already feel the dark cloud of my mood, dispersed by her infectious joviality. "Well, this might sound like a crazy idea, but it seems crazy is quite the theme, but basically, we had a footman leave without serving his notice, so we are searching for a replacement". "A footman?" I asked. "Yes, basically, like a waiter in the big house. I mean responsibilities wise, they just serve meals, and do what Mr Organ, our butler, tells you to do". I couldn't believe people still had butlers, I thought this belonged to the past, to the realms of books and films. She went on. "I know you are searching for work, so I thought you might as well work here. Obviously there are a few things we need to organise, such as the job interview with my dad. He's okay really but can be quite a thorough interviewer - especially when it comes to admitting someone into the big house. Anyway, what do you think?". Her face was stone cold as she said this. For my part, I was instantly thrilled at the idea of being a footman, whatever that entailed. I tried hard to suppress my excitement, mimicking the emotionless traits of her face, as if the puppeteer drawing the strings that usually animated her had fallen asleep, failing at his task of bringing kindness to her features.

In my most casual tone, I said, " sure, why not". Feeling I was maybe down-playing it a little too much, I added. "Thanks for this, I really appreciate it". She brought me another set of clothes that afternoon, they had belonged to her brother, who sure enough was exactly the same build as me. It was a well cut, dark blue birdseye suit, with a white shirt, a light green tie and some very nice shoes. She told me she had purposefully picked the tie to not go so well with the suit, as too much style might hinder my chances of getting the job. She told me there was no chance her father would recognise the clothes. I got changed behind a banana plant and showed myself to her. She looked at me, with glowing eyes, her lips parted slightly, as if she was trying to conceal a smile. She stared at me for what felt like a little too long for our mutual comfort, and then a slight jolt shook her, as she woke up from her dream-like state. She said: "You look great! Just like Arthur. It fits you perfectly. So...I have arranged for a meeting with my father in fifteen minutes, and we need to get you out of the property and back in through the front drive. Not sure what anyone would think seeing your stroll from the south front". The south front I thought, was this what the Brits called their back garden? I decided I would ask the question later. Mixed with the enthusiasm of seeing the big house, I also didn't quite know what to think about the fact she had already arranged an interview without really asking me - I pushed these thoughts aside and got ready.

We walked down a beautiful path, lined with large cedar trees, with their brown autumn leaves. The sun was setting, turning the shades of yellow and brown to gold and orange. It felt like I had walked into one of the Claude Laurainne paintings - from one of my favourite books - my mother had given it to me and it had found a prime spot under our coffee table. She told me she was going to head back home, gave me instructions, wished me good luck and left me. So off I went, in my perfect suit, a new man, with these trees scattering their leaves beside me, as if I was walking out of the church on my wedding day. I felt like a new man.

When I walked through the tall Iron gates, which were framed by two little houses, even with what Lily had told me, I wasn't quite ready for the sight - what I was looking at was more of a palace than a house. The long drive to the house offered a full view of its colossal facade. Lily had prepared me with a back story of what to say in the interview, and a little about the house itself, while failing to mention its sheer scale. It was called Lymington Hall and was built in the early 18th century in a Neoclassical style, by Viscount Lymington, who was the father of the Earl of Portsmouth, the house had then been sold to the family and passed down from generation to generation for the last hundred and fifteen years. It was not only large but very well proportioned. It had the same main portico with four huge columns and a large pediment than the greenhouse, but the house was Palladian architecture on steroids. The portico had two wings spreading on either side, built in a yellow stone, with a row of large windows on the piano nobile, set above a foundation of heavy rustication, every window was adorned with their own little pediment and framed by smaller, high relief columns. The second floor had smaller, less ornate windows. Surprisingly, you couldn't even see the roof, as it seemed to be hidden by a long balustrade, punctuated by stone statues and vases. It was mind blowing to think that this was a privately owned house. The scale of it all started to make me feel nauseous at the idea of meeting the man that did. This Lord wasn't born with a golden spoon in his mouth, he was born with Marie Antoinette's entire state dinner set, and unfortunately for my interview, it was likely it had been placed up his arse rather than in his mouth.

I walked up the obnoxiously large steps, and when I approached the huge black door, which must have been at least twice my size, it opened magically, revealing a young man in a Napoleonic looking uniform behind it. I put my hand out to shake his, but he just looked at me in utter shock. That's when I first met Mr Organ, or the Wart as they would later teach me to call him. He came straight to me, across the vast lobby. "So, you must be Nicolas Popov?" he said, in the most old fashioned British accent I had ever heard. He had a deep, dry voice, it felt cold and unfriendly. The words were pronounced from a mouth which seemed to be tightly closed, set above a chin that was facing upwards, as if he was scared of revealing a double chin, it gave him an air of unfounded superiority. Just like his chin, he had unusually thick eyebrows, as wide as a thumb, which protruded upwards - making him look slightly like an owl. He must have been about sixty, and was also blessed with a very large thin nose, with a great big boil on the side of it.

"Yes, that's me," I answered, offering my hand again. He shook it reluctantly, and in a weirdly soft way, as if he just didn't want to give me the satisfaction of a warm handshake. He stated, in a tone that you would expect to announce the death of a king. "Lord Mounthaven is ready...please, follow me". We walked through a couple of beautiful rooms, each one larger than the other, the furniture was beautiful. The various rooms we passed had a different colour palette, one was burgundy red, the next olive green and so on. I stared up at the gilded ceilings. My mouth opened in ore, nearly forgetting I was heading to an interview that would decide my fate. We eventually got to another large intimidating door, which Mr Organ knocked on slowly but firmly. After a "come in " could be heard from behind it, he opened it, ushering me in by flicking his head. There I stood, in this large rectangular room, the door closing behind me. Books of all colours were neatly arranged in long lines, encapsulated by beautiful woodwork which rose all the way up to the high ceiling.

Lord Mountbottom remained behind his desk, his back to the large window, still visibly occupied by his work. After a few long, uncomfortable seconds of me standing there, he looked up. I don't know what went through his mind but he looked shocked. He stared at me, his mouth slightly open, his eyes ajar, as if his facial expression was frozen in time. He didn't stand up and didn't say anything. He quickly reclaimed his composure and scrutinised me. Looking at me from top to bottom. It made me feel naked, in that moment I felt he had guessed I was a fraud, his gaze stripping my suit and seeing my naked truth.

He then pronounced, in what was a soft, deep, yet commanding voice, "well, what a timely discovery". I had no idea what that meant and I also didn't really know what to say. So as I had stupid habit of doing in these cases, I said the greatest platitude. "Nice to meet you my Lord", which Lily told me was how he was to be addressed even though his real name was Bertie, short for Osbert. "It's a beautiful house". He didn't say anything and just kept staring at me. He then asked. "How old are you then Nicolas?". "I'm twenty four, " I answered. He drew a paper from a draw and then complimented me on my CV, which took me by surprise as I hadn't provided one. Lily must have made one up, again without telling me - I got a little worried, if he asked me any questions about it, I would have no idea what to answer. Thankfully rather than asking any questions, he just said. "My daughter recommended you, I hear you just wanted a change from the Badmingtons, which I can understand." He grinned sarcastically as he said this last bit. "Anyway, you come recommended by Lily, so I'll save us both some time by giving you a two week trial period. When can you start?" I was quite shocked at how easy this had turned out, what seemed like an impossible mountain to climb was instantly reduced to a pile of golden sand. "Now, " I said. He looked at me, slightly surprised. Then stood up, called for Mr Organ, which he referred simply as "Organ". And declared to the man. "Popov will be starting tonight, if you would be so kind as to show him around and familiarise him with the house". "Yes my Lord " he answered. Showing me the door with his impossibly long and rigid arm.

I was shown to my room which was perched on the rooftop. We reached it after climbing two well hidden sets of windy staircases and a few long corridors. It was about six square metres, had a little bed and a cupboard to one side, and a roof window to the other. The ceiling was low, which made it feel warm and **cosy.** Within the immense context of the house, it felt deliberately small - but this served me well, I found those large rooms cold and intimidating, and compared to my recent sleeping arrangements, this felt like a little corner of peace. I opened the cupboard to find the same Napoleonic uniform the servant at the door had worn. It was a red tailcoat with very wide white lapels and silver buttons going all the way down from the collar to the waist. The waistcoat was a light cream colour and the trousers were black. I was pretty excited at the idea of putting it on, my dream of coming to England was materialising itself into a stereotype that even the wildest imagination could not invent. I sat on my bed, feeling relieved while reflecting on how crazy the last few days had been. It was crazy to think that I went from my town in Siberia to being a footman in this vaste house that belonged to a Tolstoy novel. I had also finally told my fathers secret, I had completed his last wish. Although Lily didn't seem convinced; now I had to get someone to actually believe me.

The next five days were punctuated by my new duties as a footman. It all went rather well, not being too hard, just a lot of etiquette to abide with. This ended up being quite exausting, as getting anything wrong would lead to my instant dismissal. I'm usually not one to stress out when learning new things, or doing something for the first time, but I was so unfamiliar to the nature of these potential mistakes, that I was worried they would creep up on me. This didn't affect my general composure, other than the one time I very nearly slightly panicked. That was just before my first shift, when I was faced with the challenge of having to wrestle with my white bow tie and submit it into a perfect bow. The ones I had used in the past, were simply clipped on and, voila. These were basically just a long piece of fabric and I had no idea where to start. I had already put on the rest of my tight fitting uniform, and tried again and again to make a knot that looked somewhat okay. The fact I had to do it in a mirror, meant all my gestures were inverted, my head started spinning, my arms felt numb due to my blood struggling to get through the tight sleeves of the jacket and, despite the fresh temperatures, sweat pearled on my forehead - I have to say, I got in a bit of a state. Considering I was supposed to have previous experience as a footman, asking help was not ideal, but I got desperate. This led to me knocking on a neighbouring room, begging for help, which is when I first properly met Billy. He managed to teach me how to do it, correcting me as I practised on tying it around my leg. My attempts were so pathetic and time was running out, so he had to tie it for me. I promised to practise later that evening and left feeling like a child. How tying a knot could be so difficult was beyond me. Billy was a lovely, simple chap, clearly finding my incompetence amazing, he later filled me in on all the gossip of the house - he was the one to tell me everyone called the butler "the Wart" due to the giant boil on his nose and so on. After each shift, I would get back to my room, tired with my feet aching from spending the day standing on them. I would then lie in bed, with no book to read, no phone, left to the mercy of my thoughts. I was desperate for a book to accompany me in my solitude, but I felt that asking to borrow one would raise questions, so I just lied on my bed, with nothing to distract me from my thoughts. These contemplations would turn to rumination, presided by the memory of Lily, who I hadn't seen since she left me walk down that path five days ago. Was she worried or even embarrassed to be seen speaking to me? Would this raise questions, or was I just not at the top of her priority list? It was strange as Lily didn't strike me as the kind of person that cares what people think of her, but it seemed like she had just vanished in thin air, I never bumped into her, never saw her when serving breakfast, lunch or dinner. Maybe she had her own apartment in the house. I also felt very confused about how to interpret those days we spent together. In some ways I missed the humid warmth of my cristal palace. She had been unbelievably mean in calling me a deserter, the words still lingered in my gut like shards of bamboo. I hoped the word deserter in the English language didn't have such bad connotations as it did in Russian, although I was pretty sure it did. On the one hand, she has been so good to me, saving me from my desolated state, getting me a job, and going to the extent of writing up a fake CV for me. These facts could not be ignored. In some ways I really regretted telling her my fathers secret. It had led her to think I was some kind of madman. On the other hand, it was pretty unusual to get a mandmann work in your family home. The thoughts swirled around, transforming my brain into what felt like a giant sinkhole, spinning again and again, sucking my usual unwavering positivity in its swell. I tried my best to keep her out of my mind. But there were little distractions and my mind always came back to Lily's enigmatic behaviour. It was as if forcing her out of my brain was making her more present. The effort this process entailed was exhausting. It was becoming an obsession.

I also made friends with other members of staff that week, notably Billy who we called Billy Boy, and Madame Boulet, the French cook. The latter was a soft and caring woman with a great sense of humour. She would put aside some nice meat which was left on plates returning from the dining room. I have never minded eating leftovers and just like Madame Boulet, I hate to see food go to waste. I had lost quite a bit of weight during the army and my travels. I have never been fat, so the weight loss was especially visible on my chest, back muscles and biceps. Eating all that meat was making my Napoleonic suit increasingly tight. I actually ended up tearing the sleeve of one of my white shirts, ironically, as I was stuffing a piece of lamb in my mouth. No one saw and I didn't tell anyone, so I was obliged to keep the red tailcoat on. The shifts were long and tiring but time flowed by; I was being well paid, well fed and was sleeping in a warm bed. I felt grateful for my change in fortune.

Chapter Four

Food and Thought

It was three in the afternoon and I was on my two hour break, before having to serve tea in the library at five - so I was lying on my bed giving my sore feet a rest. Unexpectedly someone knocked on my door, so I said "Come In". I expected to see Billy, but it wasn't; it was Lily! She came in with a broad smile, like an angel delivering a blessing. It was a confident, reassuring smile; it told me that she was delighted to see me again. I was so surprised that I just froze, gazing at her, my mouth wide open like a goldfish, my mind struggling to process her sudden apparition. The shock then gave place to embarrassment, as I was wearing my torn shirt. "Lily!" I finally said, going as red as my tailcoat, "sorry, I really didn't expect you to come up here". She laughed, "I can tell you didn't expect me Nick, you look like you've seen a ghost...The uniform suits you well, pretty funny to see you in it". I didn't quite know what she meant by "quite funny" but she didn't mention the fact I had managed to ruin the shirt in a few days. "How have you been getting on?" she asked. "Well I guess I haven't been fired yet". I said, with my RUssian bluntness. She came to sit next to me on the bed and asked me all sorts of questions about the last few days. She told me she had been up to Bath for the week, doing her best to work on her dissertation. She admitted that this had not been so successful, despite the long hours spent in the library. "Why so? Are you struggling to get started?" I asked. "Well I ended up getting slightly sidetracked on my reading. You'll find this funny, but I ended up reading about physics all week rather than politics. Specifically a few books on the earth electromagnetism, solar winds and the Van Allen Belt. I have to say it's all fascinating, maybe I should have done physics rather than politics". Then she went quiet, I hoped this research had helped her to come to terms with what I had told her. She then went on, in little more than a whisper. "It has helped me contextualise the conversation we had. If your father was right about the pole shifting from Geenland to Siberia and eventually to Kazakhstan, we may very well be facing the end of our world, at least according to the books I read." So she believed it, she believed me. A huge surge of happiness made its way across my entire body; I knew she wouldn't have gone to so much trouble researching it all for an entire week, if she had thought I couldn't be trusted. "So you believe me now?" I asked. She wobbled her head around, before eventually saying. "The theory is right, but I'm still finding it hard to digest. I'm not a physics professor and just read a few books. I mean, this is all based on the electromagnetic pole being in Siberia at the moment and shifting towards Kazakhstan, all the books I read stipulate it's still very much in the middle of Greenland. To be honest, I find it hard to imagine people wouldn't have noticed, it would be pretty easy to get such data, surely, we would just need to measure the electromagnetic current exiting from Greenland versus the one in Arkhangelsk". She was of course right, my fathers finding would have been very easy for anyone else to discover. But this did entail searching in the right place. Of course she was welcome to go out and do so herself, but for my part, I had no passport so couldn't travel. Besides, my father had been taking these measurements for the last twenty or so years, so the idea of going out to verify his finding also felt pointless. Anyway, returning to Russia was not on the cards.

She looked at me as if trying to read my thoughts. "What are you planning to do with what your father told you? I mean, should we tell people?". Surprisingly, it hadn't even crossed my mind. I had been doing my best to stay alive these last few weeks, so that I could pass this information on. The thought that once I had passed it on, to someone outside of Russia (completing my duty in some sorts), that we would have to decide whether to tell the masses or not, came as a surprise. It felt as if this was beyond my job description. I turned around to look into her eyes and admitted, "I don't know really...do you think we should tell people?", she pondered this question before answering, a few seconds later. "I believe people have the right to know the truth. My father is an MP at the house of Lords, maybe we can convince him to discuss it in parliament". - "And how do we tell him? He currently thinks I'm a footman, wouldn't it be a little odd if we suddenly tell him I'm a runaway Russian soldier?". She looked at me, pausing to give this a little thought. "The fact you're Russian is not going to make things easier, he's not much of a fan of Russians at the moment, I'll have to find a way of telling him, but I don't see a way around involving you - it would jeopardise our chances of him taking it seriously". She was right, but this also meant risking my current job. "I agree" I said, "but involving me will likely cost me my position". She looked at me, as if surprised I suddenly cared so much about being a footman. "I think your job isn't as important as letting the world know that they are all going to die in the next ten years". Easy for her to say I thought, this would be the end of my work and relative comfort here, but I knew she was right - I had to put my personal interests aside. She stood up, and said, "Okay then, I'm going to find a way of telling him about this and I'll see you around, goodbye", and she walked out of my tiny bedroom. I sat there, admiring the way she made up her mind and the decisiveness in her decision making.

The next time I saw her was at dinner, I fulfilled my duties, serving the family with my usual discretion, like a ghost hovering behind them. She didn't even exchange eye contact. She acted as a stranger, so I followed suit. Later that night, I stayed up, sat on my small bed, waiting in hope that she would pay me a visit. She didn't. She was the daughter of a lord, I was a footman, why would she bother climbing those stairs. I felt so alone that night - tortured by the realisation that I had no one left on this planet that really loved me, my only friend other than books had been my father and now he was gone. The tormented loneliness of my soul drove me to spite and anger, for a moment I felt somewhat comforted by the fact that everyone would die in ten years. The lack of love lives to nurture new evil.

At about eleven the next morning, I heard the Wart bellow my name through the kitchen. He came to tell me I was "required for an audience". Not knowing what that meant, but knowing it was bad, I just followed him, not bothering to ask why. He had this ability to bring me back to my early school days. I walked a few paces behind him down the long corridors of the ground floor, until it was clear we were heading to the library, where Lord Mountbottom worked. After the usual knock and invitation to enter, I was drawn into the room. This time, Lord Mounthaven was not behind his desk, he was sitting on a large leather sofa. To my great surprise, Lily was sitting on the other one, just four feet away from him. They were both staring at me. I could tell that Lily wasn't looking her usual confident self, as for Lord Mounthaven or Bertie as a normal person would want to be called, he looked like a spoiled boy who had been refused an ice cream, the fact the expression belonged to him though, made him all the more threatening. His eyebrows were lowered, his arms crossed. He sat back on his sofa, looking straight into my eyes. I looked at Lily for reassurance, but her expression seemed to tell me, "It's in your hands now, don't trip, he's in a bad mood". After this staring game had lasted long enough, Bertie said, "So, I have been told that you're an imposter, a Russian soldier, or shall I say a deserter and, first class liar". He said this slowly, every word weighed to hit me with a terrible impact. He continued, "I demand an explanation for you coming into this house, lying to Lily, as well as the rest of us, and taking advantage of our hospitality". I felt like asking what he meant about lying to Lily and taking advantage of them, considering I had been working over fourteen hour days, but I decided against it. Instead, I looked at him, and asked: "Do you know why I'm here?". He was slightly taken aback as to the frontal way I had pronounced this sentence but decided to ignore it and answered, "Please, go ahead, I feel it's just the time to elucidate your presence here". Lily gave me an encouraging smile. I did my best to calm my nerves and said, with more confidence than I actually had, "I will tell you my story, from the beginning, but you have to bear with me, and please, do not interrupt till I'm finished". He nodded in an accent. I inspired a long breath and started my long monologue.

After I had told him the entire story, still standing up, both of them just sat there in silence. Lily looked at me with a slight grin on her face, which may even have been interpreted as a look of pride, as if to say that I did well. He wasn't looking at me though, his eyes were unfocused, they were dotting around, animated by a strong brain in full spin. When his eyes eventually stabilised, they settled on me. "Listen carefully young man" he said, "I want you to go back up to your room, get out of that uniform and pack your bags. You are no longer working for this house. You stay up there and wait till I call for you. If we catch you trying to leave, I'll let the dogs out on you. You understand?". "Yes my Lord" I said, and took my leave. As I ran up to my room, I could feel a poisonous rise of anger paving its way through my body. I waited in my room and got into Arthur's blue birdseye suit. I sat there, feeling slightly sick. My stomach felt hollow. I was tired of people not believing me. I was fed up that each time something was going somewhat in the right direction, I was just ruthlessly taken away from me. It made me think of the myth of Sisyphus who pushes that huge rock up a mountain, to just see it roll straight back to the bottom. It all made me wish I had escaped while I was still in my cristal palace. I was now under house arrest. My room suddenly felt like a prison cell. Bertie was likely going to call the Police, and I would be on the next plane home. Although I hated indulging in self-pity, which I have always considered to be deeply unproductive, I didn't have the strength to resist it and found myself indulging in the darkness of my thoughts; the truth was, I had nothing more to be positive about. I lay on my bed, in a foetal position, paralysed by a feeling of betrayal. Yearning for a comforting I knew would never come.

Somehow I managed to fall into a deep sleep, maybe defeatism got hold of me, plunging me into a place where we can't feel pain. My slumber was interrupted by a knock. Suddenly my muscles tensed, preparing me for fight or flight. Expecting police officers to walk in, I readied myself, revising our military training in my head. Knee to the balls, kick to the face followed by violent kicks to the ribs and, make sure they stay down. I waited tensely to jump into action, but it was the Wart that walked in. As soon as I saw him I started to relax. Other than his aura of superiority, he was a harmless man. He asked me to follow him back to the library. As I walked in, Bertie was pacing about, with Lily sitting in the same position as she had a few hours ago. Bertie thanked the Wart and asked him, to my great surprise, to serve us three Whiskeys, before apologising in a sarcastic tone that they didn't serve vodka in this house. The Wart handed a heavy crystal tumbler while trying hard to conceal his surprise, he was evidently as unaware as I was about what was happening. He gave me a smaller portion of the golden liquid than Lily and Bertie, I was convinced this was to serve as a reminder of my position. Bertie asked the Wart to take his leave, after which he said to me, "I have invited an old friend to dinner. His name is Professor Neumann, he used to be a Physics professor at Oxford. You too are to be our guest tonight. The staff will be surprised, which is why Mr Organ will tell them that you are a friend of Lily's who's studying at the Royal Agricultural College, and doing some research on the dynamics of running a large country estate, I'll make sure I tell him before dinner". I was thunderstruck, I wasn't going back to Russia today, I nodded stupidly in assent. He continued, "we need to establish whether what you have told us is true, hopefully, Professor Neumann can help us with this. If it turns out to be a lie, I'll make sure you're sent straight back to your filthy country, in the meantime, you'll have the benefit of the doubt". Lily said, looking at Bertie - "my father wants to say that you're welcome to stay until we know what to do with this information. I will ask Billy to prepare you another room, so as to not further confuse the staff". I hated the idea of Billy preparing a room for me but decided not to question these arrangements. Bertie then said, "Now please sit down Nicolas, I'd appreciate it if you told us a little more about yourself," he realised he may have been a little too kind so added, "so that I don't have to have a stranger at my table". I sat down, on the large leather sofa that was pointed to me, I told them about my parents, the way we had moved away to Siberia, the obsession with the English language and demos, and the way I had landed here. He asked me all sorts of questions. It felt slightly like I was in an interrogation. He kept asking quite bizarre questions as if trying to catch me out. He seemed especially surprised that a Russian could speak such good English, but I soon relaxed, happy to be telling the truth about myself. "So do you think Putin has a terminal illness? He asked. "Well, I really don't know" I answered, "but it seems that regardless if the rumour is out there, it's either because he is, or because people would like him to be. On the one hand, you have to consider that in Russia, rumours come from the top, so it would be powerful Russians that want him terminally ill. On the other hand, you can't compare Putin to a western leader. What I mean by this is, is that he doesn't need widespread support, he just needs power. He is Russian and has in many ways reinstated Russian imperialism. He's at the top of this new order, he's our new Tsar; with absolute power. Regardless of if people want him gone, his grip on power remains so strong, that I feel it is unlikely the crown will be passed on before his death". He looked at me, with a look that hinted he was satisfied with my analysis and said:

"I hate to think how much damage he will do in the remaining time he's in power". "Yes" I answered, "I share the same fears as you, but he destroys to rebuild. He destroyed the Yeltsin Capitalist order to rebuild the empire, again, I hate the way he has done this - however, he still has a very strong following at home, people in Russia love what he has rebuilt, not so much our generation who have been brought up in big cities, or who have spent time abroad, but in general, especially in rural areas, people love him - they remember how hard the 90's where and see him as the one that saved Russia from anarchy". Lily added, "I think there's also some evidence for him being responsible for quite a lot of the mess in those years. We more or less know that Putin and his cronies were responsible for the Beslan school attack". I had heard about this and wiggled my head in assent. "What was that already?" asked Bertie.

I answered "A group of Chenchenians took a school by force, kept about a thousand people hostage for two days, after which the Russian special forces went in, it led to 330 people dying, mostly children. I remember following it all on the television, I must have been thirteen or something". "And what does this have to do with Putin?" Bertie asked.

"Well, there's evidence tying the insurgents to Putin, we think he did this in order to justify the Chechen war, rally the Russian people behind a common threat and centralise power, and this isn't the only example of him orchestrating terrorist attacks".

Bertie inspired loudly through his teeth, and said. "The good old politics of fear...I guess Thatcher did the same with the Falklands war". Lily added "and the Americans with Al-Qaeda". Bertie reclined in his armchair and said, "well with the death of political utopia at the end of the cold war, governments have to find a way of creating a common cause. Both of you are young, and might not appreciate this but, to maintain our geopolitical position, it is a necessary evil - that's why Britain needs to sell weapons". I wasn't too sure about this, I didn't believe that we needed to impose our position in the world through selling weapons or waging war. I strongly believed that democracy had spread in the same way we had, through Darwinism; becoming the best way to manage a country. It had basically survived against other ways of ruling. As if he read my mind, Bertie said: "We need to remember that democracy has only survived other regimes, such as fascism, through the fact we defended it, and we defended it with brute force. If we just sit there, talking, with no actual power to back the political statements we make, we won't be listened to, that's why we can't just let Putin invade Ukraine".

I asked him "do you think people look up to the US's foreign policy because they have a massive army?". Lily said, "Well I kind of agree with my father, people may not think much of their policy, but they certainly listen carefully, I mean, if they don't and the CIA gets involved, they just go in assassinating whoever opposes the US agenda". We kept on this topic for a while, I could tell that I was slowly rising in Bertie's esteem, and this seemed to make Lily quite happy. I enjoyed debating, especially when everyone was contributing, adding information, without getting overheated or upset. I was later shown to my room by Billy, who didn't ask any questions but seemed happy for me. I felt like saying something to him to explain this odd situation, but he didn't really let me, he even had a slight grin on the end of his lip, so I just thanked him for his friendship. I had an impression that he knew my story didn't fit from the start, as I couldn't tie a bow tie and didn't have a single possession to move into my new room; I liked the way he didn't ask questions. He left me alone in the big room, after giving me a little, sarcastic bow. I got ready for dinner, which was more of a psychological task as I was already wearing my best and only suit.

I walked into the drawing room, which I knew was where we met for a few drinks, before moving to the dining room to eat. Professor

Neumann was already there, he stood up immediately with surprising energy to greet me. He was a small old man, maybe around the age of eighty, with no hair. His head seemed too large for the rest of round body, making it look like someone had balanced an egg on a jacket potato. He smiled at me with his beady eyes. I instantly took a liking to him. Maybe it was the kindness in his beady eyes, the little circular glasses perched on his nose, or the wrinkles that served as evidence of years of smiling; he instantly put me at ease. He was wearing a black tuxedo, with an impeccably executed bow tie, which I gave him a lot of credit for; knowing just how much practice must have gone into achieving such perfection.

He asked me about where I came from, to which I answered carefully, not revealing too much. I told him I was Russian and had studied politics. I wasn't sure what he knew so, purposefully didn't give too much away. He eventually said "I hear your father was a Physics professor, just like me", making me realise that he had clearly been given a detailed overview of my life by Bertie. Lily joined us, she was wearing the most beautiful dress. It was a champagne coloured silk, reflecting hues of orange and yellow as she elegantly walked toward me. She gave me a short kiss on the cheek, doing the same to Professor Neumann, who she called George. He said: "I gather we are here to discuss what appears to be a most upsetting subject". I was somewhat shocked and relieved to hear him say this. It meant that he took the narrative seriously, and probably had a good idea of it being the truth. The tone he pronounced that sentence was also surprising, he said it in a matter of fact way, as if discussing oncoming bad weather. Bertie then walked into the room, with his wife, Lady Katherine Mounthaven. She was also a very beautiful woman, she was the regal incarnation of severity and elegance. Her face never seemed to give much away, in some ways it felt quite Russian, although the stillness of expression may have been as a result of an abuse of botox. She was so thin that she could have looked slightly ill if it wasn't for her confident stride and the way she carried her head. It was as if some imaginary person was dangling her by a cable, set at the top of her head, extending and floating her around the room. Bertie seemed in strong spirits, and greeted Professor Neumann with a warm embrace, patting him on the back. Again, I found myself surprised, they were clearly old friends but I hadn't been expecting such warmth from him, especially in such a conservative setting. Maybe the Whiskey had made its way to find the kind child that was deep within him. Lady Katherine glanced at me, and then towards Professor Neumann and said "good evening". She clearly wasn't going to treat me any differently than when I was her footman. She then added "I see you have already met Lily's friend Nicolas. You know Lily found him hiding away in our greenhouse". Her tone was icy, as if to remind everyone that I belonged to a pile of mud. Bertie glanced at her, as if a little taken aback by her comment; was he pleading for her to be a little kinder to me? Professor Neumann, then said, turning to me with his caring eyes "I know, you must have been through a lot, young boy, I have to say I'm very impressed at the way you managed to escape, a demonstration of true bravery and resilience". Lady Katherine didn't seem as amused as Lily; who clearly admired how skillfully Professor Neumann had turned her malice into a compliment. He then said "I'm so sorry to hear about your father, it must be horrible for you". Realising he must know my entire life story, I answered "to be honest, I feel that wherever he is, he feels he has completed his life mission. I'm not even sure he wanted to live much longer without my mother. I'm sure he'd be very happy to see how generous and understanding the Mounthavens have been towards me"; feeling like a teacher's pet, I looked towards Lady Katherine, to see whether this petty compliment had landed. Unsurprisingly, she just wore the same, emotionless face; as if she was one of those ladies taking part in the Venetian carnival, beautifully dressed, but faceless. Professor Neumann started asking me all sorts of questions about Russia, with Bertie and Lily adding comments and asking further questions. Lady Katherine didn't seem to be thrilled at the fact I was the centre of attention and decided not to take part in our conversations, excusing herself to "powder her nose" an expression which left me puzzled. For a second, an image of her snorting a line of Cocaine came to my mind, but I quickly chased the thought out of my mind. The discussion continued - I was starting to enjoy myself. As we were about to sit down and the rest of the party went through the large doors to the dining room, Lily took my hand and pulled me back. She played with my fingers with her ten little chubby extremities. The tips of my fingers were crying with pleasure, my nerves sent bolts of fire up to my brain, the tingling sensations were then reverberated down my spine, I felt warmth my stomach, as if hot air was blowing through me; I left that room to enter a space of enhanced pleasure and sensitivity. Until she spoke to say "you're doing very well, I think my father is starting to like you." This brought me back to the present, leaving me with the feeling that I was her boyfriend, meeting her parents for the first time. I thoroughly loved this idea; I loved the way she had touched my hand - the freedom she had over my body.

I answered "It doesn't seem your mother is my biggest fan". "Well, I'm not sure she's too keen on anything that doesn't involve dogs or horses" she said, and then looked at our tangled fingers and said "sorry, I'm a very tactile person, I hope you don't mind". I smiled, and then felt blood rushing to my cheeks, I went bright purple - this gesture of tenderness that had seemed so natural a second ago, suddenly made me feel deeply embarrassed; I said "no, I don't mind at all, I'm very tactile too", this wasn't true, at least until now.

We walked through the giant doors to the dining room. As I took my seat, I found myself staring at a multitude of different forks, knives and spoons. A beautiful looking starter had already been placed in the middle of the rows of silver soldiers - I knew I would have to attack the plate with them, but was oblivious as to which ones to use. I covertly observed Lady Katherine and saw that she had picked up the smaller pieces of silverware, which were placed outside. The dinner was delicious, and it was good to have first picks rather than eating the leftovers. I also enjoyed the amusing challenge of navigating British etiquette without being noticeably a clear amateur; however, the conversation was not as exciting as it had been in the drawing room. It was hard not to blame Lady Katherine for this; she was at the head of the table and was ensuring all conversation revolved around her. She would direct questions to Lily, Professor Neumann or her husband, initiating a discussion. As soon as it was out of her depth, or getting too technical, she would switch topics by asking another question, usually completely unrelated to the last. I admired how skillful she was at ensuring the largest range of topics were explored, without us ever getting the chance to discuss anything in depth. Small talk could not have been better illustrated than in this moment. Naturally, she made a point of not addressing any of her questions to me. There were a few attempts from Lily and Professor Neumann to include me, as they asked for my opinion on a certain question, but after she had listened to my answer - looking utterly bored, she would swiftly change topic; It was like watching a television which automatically changed channels every two minutes. We ended the meal with the most amazing orange sorbet; I had never tasted such a thing and I was instantly convinced it was the best ice cream I had ever tasted. The Wart then came in declaring: "tea and drinks have been served". We all stood up, and to my pleasant surprise, Lady Kathernie said to Bertie: "I'm feeling rather tired, do you mind if I leave you to it?", and then turned to the rest of us adding; "please excuse me, I'll leave you to discuss the apocalypse, I don't feel too well tonight, have a lovely evening". We all said our goodbyes to her, all felt slightly childish as if we were playing some imaginary game which she was too grown up for. Despite her sarcasm, everyone seemed relieved to see her go.

No tea was served, as everyone decided the topic was best paired with Whiskey. We opened a bottle of Jura, which was very smoky. I had never had such a taste in my mouth and I found it delicious. Bertie started us off by saying. "Firstly, I would appreciate it if George could give us his professional opinion on the situation".

After a quick sip of his drink, Professor Neumann stood up and straightened his jacket: "Sure, happy to offer my opinion. I have done some preliminary research, but since you told me all of this yesterday, I will need more time in order to reach any scientific conclusions. Nevertheless, I can confirm that the electromagnetic extremity of the pole is currently in Siberia and not in Greenland. So in this sense Nicolas is right. How this hasn't come to our attention before, baffles me, as it's very easy to measure this with a magnetometer. I was actually quite lucky that the Hampshire Observatory happens to have one".

He took a deep breath and pushed on: "As for being certain that the extremity is moving the Kazakhstan, well we will need more readings, over a period of a minimum of a month, to prove it's still moving. In this sense, we need to study at which velocity it is progressing and, with those readings we can extrapolate the data in order to calculate when the pole will be near Kazakhstan. As we don't have this data, I can only speculate what would happen, based on the scenario Nicolas has described to us. Now, if it happens to be correct and the pole ends up in Kazakhstan in ten years time, well...". He slightly tilted his head backwards and looked at me "In theory you're right Nicolas. If the location of our electromagnetic pole reaches Kazakhstan, well...let's say that global warming will take on a whole new meaning".

Bertie asked: "Could you give me a better understanding of what an electromagnetic pole is?"

"Sure, it's quite simple really. Basically the matter that makes up our planet is slightly charged with electrons, these electrons are drawn to the iron core of the earth. They all come together to form a current that flows from the south pole, to the north pole and then the current splits to go outwards to either side of our atmosphere. It then goes round the atmosphere, to reenter the earth on the south pole. It's an endless circular motion that's essential in stabilising our atmosphere. It's crucial to life on earth".

Lily asked: "What do you mean George? Does this mean we have no chance of survival?".

He answered, "My dear Lily, I am a mere retired Physics professor, unfortunately I have no idea of whether survival would be possible if such an event were to happen. I can only use my knowledge of the laws of Physics to predict the effect this would have on our planet but only from a theoretical perspective. You have men like Elon Musk who claim they are about to send people to populate Mars". He sat down as if defeated, like an inflatable snowman slowly deflating, punctured by a long winter.

He continued: "Without an electromagnetic field or an ozone layer, we would be living in quite similar conditions to those we have observed on Mars; our best and possibly only chances of survival would be to go underground. We would need large artificial farms, vast amounts of fresh water and a myriad of other essentials for human survival."

He tilted his head, his usual jovial intonation had faded away, giving way to a slow, monotone voice, void of passion or excitement. "I don't work for SpaceX, but I have friends that do or have done, they say that it's all a fantasy and very far from being a reality, just the dream of a megalomaniac. The only thing we are pretty sure of, is that there is no life on Mars. There may have been in the past, it's even quite likely, but right now, it's not a place that can sustain life. The hurdles we would need to surmount in order to do so are massive and, there is a clear difference in sending people up there to do some research and actually leaving them out there to survive. All that to say that I'm not too optimistic regarding human survival on earth based on the conditions Nicolas has described". This statement was followed by a long silence. I glanced at Lily with the corner of my eye, her light brown eyes were dancing around, their colour had turned to gold. They were like the flaming torch - protecting her against some looming predator.

Professor Neumanne eyes had a greatly contrasting expression, which really did not inspire confidence, it was as if the genius that inhabited his brain had left, leaving his eyes vacant. He was staring at his Whiskey glass, as if hypnotised by it.

Bertie was also feeling a little distressed, his head was bobbing around lightly as if he was trying to gently shake sense into his thoughts; it seemed to work as he was the first to break the silence. "But surely if we know that humanity and our entire ecosystem is at such a risk, we will invest everything we have, and build these tunnels, or find some kind of solution, I mean we have been through ice ages, we have always adapted - humans will adapt to any environment".

Professor Neumann answered, in the same slow uninspiring tone, "well I'm not so sure. Maybe my age has led me to doubt humanity's ability to come together, but firstly you would have to get people to believe you - which is no easy task these days, and secondly we aren't looking at an ice age here". I was with him on this point, it seemed people really just wanted to hear what they wanted these days, this fear of the truth was also likely responsible for the disappearance of my father. People have preferred to lock up the truth rather than come to terms with it ever since the wheel was invented.

He then added, with a bit more vigour in his voice, "thirdly, there is no way we are saving eight billion people by putting them into tunnels, so telling people would likely not be the right course of action". I hadn't thought about this, but he was likely right.

Lily interjected to ask "So you mean that people won't believe the world is ending if we tell them, and even if they do believe us, they will quickly realise they can't be saved?".

I hadn't spoken much so far, but felt an urge to answer Lily's question, so I did my best to contribute by adding: "humans can get nasty when it comes to their survival. If billions suddenly start fearing for their lives and the lives of their loved ones, they will go crazy. I'm not even sure telling them the truth would be the right thing to do." I paused while images of the apocalypse, inspired by all these senseless Hollywood movies, flicked through my mind.

I said: "Just imagine the violence this could lead to, the panic and chaos. On balance, maybe this information is best kept secret, I mean to protect them".

Professor Neumann chuckled and said, "Spoken like a true Russian". He didn't laugh at his own joke, but his humorous interjection at my expense had had a lasting effect, the atmosphere was lighter, the air was thinner. Humour is like a valve, with the ability to release pressure.

He then added: "if you're proven right, Nicolas; this is more of a philosophical question than a scientific one. Basically, you're asking me if truth should be democratised, regardless of its context and impact. Now…telling someone they are going to die is tricky". He finished off his glass and continued "For example, my father died of lung cancer, forty three years ago, the doctor actually never told him he had terminal cancer; as the family, we were all told and asked to keep this horrible secret to ourselves, and hide it from him. It was horrible for us and felt like the worst betrayal. The logic behind this practice at the time was a utilitarian one, the thought that the truth would only add extra pain. Of course, we don't do this anymore, the context has changed and so have the consequences of hiding this truth". His tone had returned to its soft, didactical self. "Today we believe that if you're going to die, you should be told". This reminded me of my mother, who had always told me that life is a long preparation for your funeral. Sometimes my father would ask her where she was off to, she would answer "just going to recruit new friends for my funeral". I had found this quite funny at the time, as well as recognising the deep truth in it. The love we pick up in life is often the best quantifier of its total worth.

Bertie said:"I think it's a good thing we tell people they are going to die, the acceptance of death is the only way to live a life without fear".

Lily said: "Yes well, if only everyone was a Stoic like you, farther".

Professor Neumann said "I agree about it being the right thing to do from an individual perspective. In the case of my father dying from cancer, we should have told him. It would have helped him prepare for his death, it would have offered answers to his deteriorating health. However, if we are trying to consider the impact of releasing this truth, we have to recognise that my father was a different case for whom, in retrospect, the truth was a net benefit. In contrast we are talking about telling every human being on this planet that they are going to die in a very specific amount of time".

I agreed, the scale of this revelation was going to be the problem. The individual and the collective need to be treated differently. I felt it was nevertheless the wrong thing to keep the truth from people. I felt an urge to defend the idea of offering the truth so said, "If I was a man working a horrible job to pay for my retirement in fifteen years, I would want to know the world is ending in fifteen years". I couldn't think of anything worse than doing a horrible job until my last day alive, dreaming of a retirement that would never materialise. George Neumann responded by saying, "the thing is, without these people working these horrible jobs, the world would stop, we would plunge into anarchy, so all those retirement savings would be worthless anyway. As for telling people the truth, that they will die, well I would argue this is the only truth we all have access to, the certainty that we will, one day, die. They already have access to this truth - what we need to understand is the cost of adding a timeline to this truth".

Bertie said "I agree with you George, we need to look at this from a utiliarian's perspective. We should look at maximising the greater good, rather than telling people the truth for the sake of it".

Lily then added "Mills would say, the utilitarian ideal of capital punishment, which he was in favour of, is that suffering is always the ultimate aspect we should try to avoid. So the only justification for capital punishment in his opinion, is servitude for life; which Mill believed was worse than capital punishment. He also added the fact that people are more afraid of being killed than they are of life imprisonment, so capital punishment actually deters people from doing crime, while also minimising pain". I really didn't see how this was relevant, so asked "Sorry, what are you trying to get to?" she smiled at me - "Well I'm saying that according to Mills, imprisonment for life is worse than death. If we consider the life of the man you describe, working a horrible job until retirement - this could be considered as servitude for life, it may even be worse as its self inflicted. There has been a sharp rise in depression in our society, to give you an idea, suicide rates of young Croatians between the age of fifteen to twenty seven has increase by more than 57 percent in 2020 -

people suffer the most horrible psychological torments. Maybe an early death will relieve them from further pain". She looked into my eyes before saying "We would have to take this into account into our calculation, to define whether people are better off knowing they are all going to die, in the midst of raging chaos; or whether we should keep this secret from them. Because keeping the secret from them would involve a death after ten years of undisturbed continuation of their lives" she had argued this point quite beautifully, her lips dancing to the music of wisdom. I couldn't help but stare at her in admiration and felt a smile slowly draw itself on my face. A Russian smile is a rare thing, and worth a lot more than a British smile.

Bertie interrupted my thoughts by saying "how would you go about calculating the cost to individual lives of the economic, socio-political collapse. I mean think of everything that's around you. It would be worthless. Markets would crash, all our property in London would be worthless. This house would be worthless too".

Lily answered this "well maybe this is the real question then. What is it worth, to you, as an individual, knowing that you are going to die in ten years, compared to everything you own being destroyed. You can choose between truth and prosperity. Between the luxury of accepting your own death and the luck of having supermarket shelves well stocked. I would imagine the rich, who have more to lose, would opt for stability, while the desperate would welcome ten last years of anarchism, they would celebrate the destruction of a system that has suppressed them. We can't make these calculations based on your fear of losing the piles of capital our family has accumulated over generations - maybe those that have less to lose will react differently to their imminent death". She then turned to me and asked "what would you choose Nick?".

I knew from her direct tone that this was a test, I took my time to answer, weighing my words "I'm young and destitute, I want to live these next ten years doing as much as possible, living them to the fullest, achieving something. It's very important to me that I know my fate. I wouldn't trade knowing the date of the end of my path, as things stand today".

Bertie raised his eyebrows and interjected. "No offence Nicolas, but you are missing the point here. You are looking at this without considering the consequence of everyone else having access to the truth. You want to live your last minutes to the fullest, go travel. You won't have that opportunity if everyone knows the world is coming to an end. Your last ten years would be punctuated by violence, your travels would only reveal the worst of humanity, its horrible and omnipresent suffering".

As annoyed as I was that he had contradicted me in front of Lily, I had to agree with his point; when you hold the truth and others don't, you have a position of power over ignorance, but if the world also had access to the truth, we would all be destined to share the same suffering.

Bertie continued: "with age you build confort, you build wealth and you want peace. Life isn't necessarily about jumping out of planes, travelling and going clubbing. It's also about passing what you were given to your children..." he stopped speaking, looked at Lily, with a sudden fear in his eyes. It had just hit him, Lily was of course also going to die. There was silence in the room. The red silk walls of the large room seemed to draw in closer. I could see a slight jittering in Bertie's jaw. He sprang to his feet, as if just realising he'd been sat on a wasps nest. He looked a little confused and muttered he was sorry and needed to go to *wash his hands*. George Neumann watched him walk out, with an empathetic look drawn of his kind face. We all stayed in silence for a while, plunged in thought.

I stood up and walked around. It was quite an odd feeling to think that everyone here, as well as everyone who I had ever met would die, all together, at the same time. In a way, the fact we would all be dying together was quite reassuring. I don't know if it was the Whiskey or the hurricane of thoughts and emotions swirling in my brain but I started to feel quite dizzy. I had come to terms with the idea of my death, I just hoped it would be a painless death. It was also reassuring to know that this was a universally shared fate. Maybe this was why people committed suicide in groups. It must be one of those deeply human traits, a sort of tribalism, that accepts a common fate; helped by the departure of others to say their goodbyes. Maybe there wouldn't actually be widespread violence, maybe that this shared end would actually bring the whole of humanity together as an ultimate reminder of our equality in the face of nature.

It became clear to me that even if those so-called tunnels were an option, I would prefer to die a common death rather than live underground and be stripped of all the things I love. Maybe others would also prefer this fate rather than fighting for their salvation.

The silence was starting to make the room feel empty. As if those red walls were drawing outwards; like lung tissue in the midst of a deep inspiration.

I wanted to say something to cheer everyone up, but couldn't find anything to say. I concluded that silence was more respectful than the interference of some platitude. I sat back next to Lily, gave her my hand, which she fumbled gently. We had gotten very close lately, I was starting to get more comfortable at the idea of being so close to her, of feeling her skin against mine. She put her head against my shoulder, resting it as if the weight of these thoughts were too much for her neck muscles to handle. We stayed there. Lost in thought, transported to some far-away island, sat on a small mound that stopped us from sinking.

Chapter Five

The Rock Rolls Downhill

I was in my bed, under the heavy linen sheets when Lily knocked and then timidly came into my room, without waiting for me to invite her in. She was in a great deal of distress, she had sweat pearling on her forehead, her hair was tangled into a thick mane, falling uncontrollably over her loose white nightgown. Her breasts were free to float around and I could see her nipples protruding through the thin white cloth. She looked confused, like a scared child who's lost her mother; this only brought forward an innocence I had never seen in her, making her more sensual than ever, like a lioness that's desperate to feed her starving cubs. She told me in a low voice, truncated by sharp breaths that she had just had a terrible nightmare. In an impulse of affection for her, I jumped out of my bed and opened my arms to her, she slid herself into my embrace, our bodies interlaced and I held her close. It was the first time I had felt a body get so close to mine, not in a sexual way though as I had had girlfriends, but this was different. It was as if her body belonged there, as if the act of being so close to her had heated my blood to the right temperature, it just felt like two pieces of a jigsaw were coming together and the full picture was complete. I whispered a few reassuring words into her ears, and told her to lie on the bed. I went to put on my dressing gown as I was in underwear - I was also worried I might get an erection. As she climbed into the bed I brought up a chair by her side. Everything in my soul was begging me to climb in with her, but it felt wrong, she was too special, she was my saviour and princess and had to be treated as such. She gave me her cold hand which I warmed between my clammy palms. When she was breathing a little more normally, I asked her to describe her dream. She said in a low, scared voice: "I was lying by the lake, here at Lymington Hall, sunbathing with my friend Lottie. I couldn't quite see her face, she..." she started hyperventilating again. "Her face started melting, and then the trees all caught fire, just like that. Then my teeth started to fall out, into my hands, which were also on fire. I was melting like an icecream. I tried my best to run to the lake, but I couldn't, I was already melted to the ground, stuck there screaming, blazing up in flames. Lottie was also on fire, screaming in the most horrible way, that scream...I was so, so vivid". I tried to calm her down, saying it was just a dream. She looked me straight into the eyes beforde asking: "But is it? That's what George said would happen! Aren't we all just going to burn up in flames like that?". I told her I really didn't know and most likely nor did George Neumann, I did my best to soothe her, telling her it was just a dream, that it would all be fine. As she slowly relaxed and eventually fell into a deep sleep, a quote came to my mind, it was from a Stoic Philosopher Gaius Musonius Rufus, *"Choose to die well while you can; wait too long, and it might become impossible to do so"*.

I woke up as light started to filter in through the heavy floral curtains. Still in my chair, feeling a little confused as to where I was, I noticed Lily had already left. The thought that we had spent the night together, filled my heart with both passion and fear. The thought of it then started to make my whole body cringe, as if small shards of glass were being slipped between my ribs. My flesh felt torn apart between the hope that I would one day share a bed with Lily, and the knowledge that it was in fact impossible. I was a Russian footman and she was some sort of princess. I just sat there, on my chair, trying my best to chase her from my mind; but I just couldn't. I started getting angry at myself, I knew she didn't feel the same way as I did; it made me feel like a hot water bottle, used to provide warmth amongst this cold and humid house. It was like a demon had taken control of my brain, fermenting spiteful thoughts. I knew I needed to do something about it; I decided I was going to tell her how I felt, if she didn't like it I would leave.

I went down for breakfast and sat next to Lily. As soon as I did so, the remnants of anger I had left were diffused by her warm smile; I asked her how she felt. She said much better, and added: "Please don't get the wrong message from me entering your room last night, of course nothing happened, but I just wanted to say that I value your friendship and wouldn't want you to get the wrong message". That was it I thought, in black and white, no need to tell her about my feelings. Was I that easy to read? Could she feel me coming onto her? My neck recoiled into my shoulders, like a turtle's head. Trying to sound slightly surprised she would even draw such a conclusion, I said: "Not at all, don't be silly, I'm happy you're feeling better. I value your friendship a lot". She looked at me, plunging into the depth of my mind, she then smiled in what I can only describe as an elegant smile. One a sophisticated mother would give to a weak child, a smile that shows she knows he will never grow to become a good man. It was both sad and compassionate. I looked out of the grand windows, across the pristine lawn which was framed by a collection of different coloured trees, their foliage flooded by the clearest morning light. It was a beautiful day, without a single cloud in the sky; the light was crisp, it shone with a certain severity, bouncing off the silvery dewed grass and finding its way to my squinting eyes. "Let's go for a walk", she said.

Just before we left, we bumped into Lady Mounthaven in the great hallway, she had just come back from a horse ride and was in very high spirits; she said "Morning you two, are you off for a walk?" It was the first time she had willingly addressed me. "It's a gorgeous day out there, It's just so wonderful to be out and about on such a day, have fun!" she said in a jolly voice. She walked off and added without even turning round, her voice echoing down the hall "don't be too long, we have Father Thomas coming over for lunch". As we walked out the colossal front door, Lily explained that Father Thomas was the local priest, that he was an Anglican priest - I was surprised to hear he had a wife. I told her about the Orthodox church and we ended up talking about Rasputin. She was fascinated to hear about the religious sect he came from; the way they would have crazy orgies and do all sorts of very sinful acts. She didn't quite understand how that made sense at first, so I had to explain that they believed the more you sinned, the more you could repent, and as a result, the closer you were to god. We laughed wholeheartedly at the wonderful ways humans find to justify their vices. It was a lovely walk, we spoke about all sorts of things, but for the two topics that were governing my mind. Her feelings for me, and our imminent death.

Father Thomas was exactly what you would expect a British priest to look like. He was in his mid-fifties, had short, grey hair, a well-trimmed moustache and attractive, elegant features. He was a slim, athletic-looking man with a good posture; he was sipping a glass of cherry when we came into the living room. His handshake was warm, and he spoke to me with a soft, slow intonation. I could tell he was a great orator, one that wins arguments through carefully built debate rather than a loud overpowering voice.

I don't know if it was the winter sun, flowing through the large arched windows, the constant refills of cherry or Father Thomas' infectious positivity; but everyone was in very good spirits. Lady Mounthaven was a different person, chatting away, her face lit up with as much animation as her botox would allow. I thought it was such a shame people felt the need to make themselves look younger. She was still beautiful, but the fact she couldn't really smile with her eyes gave a certain emptiness to her animation. Although I could clearly tell she was happy, her smile still seemed to concede a deep sadness. I concluded that this was because when she smiled, the skin around her eyes would remain static; which gave her smile a sort of fakeness as if she was trying too hard to look happy. She was delighted to talk about her horses, a passion Father Thomas seemed to share with her. I asked him, while also addressing the wider group about the role of the Anglican church in Britain. Lily had already given me a crash course during our walk, so for once I didn't feel like a complete incult. Lady

Mounthaven was the one to answer most of my questions. She did so in an unusually soft tone, one which I could tell was deeply sincere, almost maternal. This sudden change in behaviour left me feeling a little uneasy.

Over lunch, just after everyone had finished eating a prawn cocktail as a starter, out of nowhere, Bertie said "Dear Father, there has been a question, which has been much discussed in this house as of late; We have been deliberating a hypothetical scenario. Purely for the fun of it; I feel you would add a most interesting angle".

I was surprised to hear him position the situation in this way, but upon seeing that Father Thomas looked quite amused, I agreed this was a rather smart play from Bertie.

Father Thomas said, "Yes, please, tell me more, I would love the opportunity to debate with a member of parliament". Bertie nodded in appreciation of this encomium and went on:

"So the world is going to end in ten years, our hypothetical scenario dictates that we will lose our atmosphere, accompanied by constant volcanic eruptions, and radiation from solar winds. This scenario leaves little hope for humanity, with a slim possibility a very select few could survive by burying themselves deep underground".

An amused smile drew itself on Father Thomas' face;

Bertie continued: "In this scenario, only the people around this table know the world will end; the dilemma I offer to you is as follows: Should we tell the rest of the population the truth? Or should we keep living our lives, keeping this horrible truth from them".

There was a moment of silence as Father Thomas gave the question some careful thought. He then asked a series of questions, such as:

"How sure are we that this will happen?" and "How long would people have to live?" and so on. I liked the way he was trying to get a full picture before choosing his stance. I would have expected him, as I imagine a priest would, to say that the truth is always the way and stubbornly stick to this concept. Instead, he came out with something quite different.

"I think I would disguise the truth, by which I mean, figure out a way to make them believe it; such as through a story. I would try to orchestrate a universal truth which offers them the guidance of this truth, without creating panic". We all looked at him, waiting for him to offer more clarity.

"I'm not sure it would be productive to offer the actual truth, as people would need some reassurance which science often fails to offer. Something more digestible...more agreeable, something in which people can find some solace".

Lady Mounthaven seemed delighted and said, "So you mean disguising the truth through a lie?". A priest saying he would happily lie to people was rather unusual.

He answered: "It depends on what you consider a lie. As an example, I believe the Bible is full of truth. It tells you "you shall love your neighbour as yourself", it offers examples of great generosity, such as the feeding of the five thousand. Jesus feeds them all with a couple of fish and a few loaves of bread". We all looked at him, trying hard to follow his thought process, "there is a lot of truth in this story, the message being that you can help everyone, regardless of the means you have, as long as you have a deep love which you are willing to share. However, the actual story is, in my opinion, a metaphor, as miracles don't happen in real life".

Lily asked: "So you would offer a metaphor for the world ending? The only thing I would point out, is that I'm not sure modern society is as credulous as they used to be over two thousand years ago".

We all nodded in agreement. He responded "Yes, you're right, and I wouldn't expect everyone to believe it. I'm not even sure what narrative I would even choose, but I would probably set out to convince all religious leaders; like the Dalai Lama, the Pope, and others, from a scientific perspective. Then, we could agree as to what narrative we should adopt".

Bertie smiled and said: "I'm not sure convincing religious leaders to come together behind a scientific truth would be an easy task. Wouldn't you say that religion and science are incompatible".

Father Thomas gave him a kind-hearted smile and said "You know I embrace science and believe it's perfectly compatible with religion. Not many people still believe in a bearded man watching us above the clouds. My interpretation is that God is the energy that has created us, he's the universe and he's nature; he's the force that drives waves to crash against the sand. To paraphrase Spinoza; *God is the infinite and the unique substance of this earth*, so I believe in science, but I don't believe in it delivering all answers".

Bertie said, "but typically, if you don't mind me saying, some rather more concrete answers than religion does".

Father Thomas was clearly enjoying this back and forth, answering with yet another smile; "Again, coming back to your original dilemma, I believe that some truths, such as that of death, are so beyond our comprehension, that embellishing them can be to the benefit of people; if we look at it from the angle of minimising suffering".

I interjected, "I agree with your interpretation of god, yet I'm not sure that telling people, who live in misery all their lives while donating their money to the church, hoping this will guarantee eternity in heaven; is fair."

Father Thomas seemed to nod in assent. "Of course, blind belief typically leads to manipulation, humans have a thirst for power and can be greedy for more of it. The Roman Catholic church was more or less founded to centralise power and have a greater control over people, at a time when different factions of catholicism were clashing violently in the Roman empire. This was however for the right reasons at the time, as they fundamentally wanted to reduce fighting between these different factions of early Catholics".

I was a little confused by his answer, so asked: "But again, I'm not sure that the argument of centralising religious power to limit religious wars is relevant today, why should we still encourage individuals to donate their wealth to the church, rather than to their children".

Thomas agreed, and he answered: "I still believe that if the individual you describe is scared enough of what comes after death to donate large sums of his income, and if his belief in religion can help reduce that fear, then this is a net reduction in suffering".

Lady Mounthaven, who had been rather quiet till now said: "Let's get back to the scenario. So you believe you can reduce the pain of death through making up a story, which you intend to make people believe, through convincing religious leaders that the world is going to end, through the use of science. So may I ask you, what would the benefit be of such a scheme?". This made me think I had quite an original priest in front of me. On the one hand, he was the worst; one could interpret his words as those of an atheist, on the other hand, you could tell he had a deep passion for god, and embraced all information that came to him.

Father Thomas replied to Katherine "In the scenario you describe, I would imagine you can't tell people the scientific truth, or their distress would lead to too much destruction. I would like to offer a narrative which can get them prepared for the truth, to get them to march together rather than fight each other - This narrative would have to offer them the truth of imminent death while not being concrete enough to drive them to panic. It would offer a way of telling the truth or offering free access to the truth, with the added benefit that, as you rightly pointed out Lily, most people wouldn't initially take it as a universal truth, they would likely interpret it as religious madness - they would have access to the truth without being forced to come to terms with it". I could see quite a few flaws in his argument, but he had gotten a step closer to telling people the truth than we had.

He continued: "The point is, these statements, made by religious leaders simultaneously would attract the attention of scientists, who would in turn prove the science and truth behind their religious statements. This would in some ways offer evidence of the initial narrative being sent by god, and add weight to whatever, the reassuring narrative we agree to release. That way, we would engineer a lie which would be the most efficient way of spreading the truth to as many people, in the healthiest way possible".

I had to admire the way religion was such a great tool for mass manipulation. Father Thomas had gone and found a strategy for the greater good. I realised that religion can offer guidance, especially in the darkest of times; it can be a tool to disguise and promote the truth in the form of a nice, digestible story. We spent the rest of the meal demonstrating all the flaws in his arguments, such as the fact it wasn't democratic; as more religious people would access the truth than atheists. It was good fun debating this topic, yet his scenario was purely theoretical, and we all found it difficult to take it seriously.

In the next few days, we spoke less about the topic, and when we did, we would treat it as the hypothetical scenario Bertie had introduced. It made the discussions a lot more light-hearted, we were all keen to come up with new solutions that could minimise pain while maximising the spread of truth. We even considered silly ideas such as kicking off a nuclear war, but in the end, no real conclusion was ever reached. There was no right answer to a problem of such dimensions; purely because although everyone would be affected in the same way, individual lives would be impacted differently. The world is unfair as it is, different people lead different lives; just like distinct things will offer them distinct pleasures; so treating a universal problem with a blanket solution is never going to be the right way, although it often seems to be the only way. If offering a truth is going to lead to greater pain and destruction than staying quiet, then maybe silence is best.

I enjoyed these debates, and gradually this large cold house felt warmer to me. The daily routine was punctuated with interesting discussions, meals and walks. The Mounthavens now treated me as an old friend, I felt like I had known them for a long time and found myself feeling very comfortable in their presence.

Unfortunately, this was not to last; it was as if an external force had decided that my place was not to be in a state of happiness, I belonged to the world of suffering and was fated to return home. The stars seemed to align to form the steel bars of my new cage.

The end of those wonderful days happened at breakfast three days after having had lunch with Father Thomas. Berties and Lily had gone shooting early that morning, at a friend's neighbouring estate. Although I had been asked to join, I politely declined as killing anything for fun made me feel a little uneasy. Besides, I had had my fill of large explosions and guns for a lifetime. I was having breakfast with Lady Mounthaven, who had taken a liking to me, naturally not as much as her favourite lurcher called Arnold, but I felt she looked at me in a similar way as she did Lily, with a slightly disinterested maternal look which quickly turned to severity if I contradicted her in any way. It was raining quite heavily that morning, which made us both feel bad for Lily and Bertie, while also bearing slight self-guilt of being rather happy at how dry we were ourselves. As soon as Billy Boy left the room to get more coffee, she shocked me by blurting out: "Nicolas, I'm sorry but your stay here has come to an end". I couldn't get myself to ask why, she added she felt I had been a wonderful guest and even apologised for her initial hostility towards me. She explained that she was going to give me four thousand pounds in cash, as my salary for my days as a footman. She told me she had already put the cash in a bag upstairs, along with some extra warm clothes and other supplies which could be helpful for my journey ahead. She then explained that I was going to have to leave in a couple of hours.

I was in such shock that I was struggling to conceal it. After a while of being silent, I managed to ask if I could wait to say goodbye to Bertie and Lily and thank them for helping me when I had been in such dire need. Her answer broke me.

She said "Nicolas, I didn't want to complicate things by telling you this, but it's Lily that has asked for you to leave. She discussed this with Bertie and me yesterday, saying that she had gone to your room a few days ago, seeking comfort after a nightmare and that you abused her trust by behaving...quite inappropriately". I froze, my initial shock gave way to utter horror. I just stared at her, my eyes bulging out of their sockets, my throat constricted; struggling for breath. I eventually managed to ask, in what sounded like a shriek; "WHAT?". Lady Mounthaven pitifully looked at me, and said, "Look, Nicolas, it's not appropriate to discuss the details. You see, I prefer not to hear your version of the ins and outs of what happened that night, all I know is that my daughter, Lily, wants you to leave this very morning and never come back". At this point, she stood, walked toward the door and when she was just about to leave, she said "Please meet me in the hall at eleven, I'll have your bag ready", and off she went, her heels echoing down the corridors.

I sat there. Alone at the breakfast table. My head was empty, I couldn't even form a thought. It was as if Katherine had pulled the ground under my feet. All the stability and comfort I had felt just moments ago had vanished - it was as if I suddenly realised that the foundations of this new life had been precariously balanced over the top of a pyramid. I walked up to my bedroom, dragging my feet up the stairs as if I was wearing armour made out of lead. I sat on my bed, not knowing what to think. Why had Lily lied about that night? Did she actually believe that I had taken advantage of her? No, nothing happened, but why lie then? I simply couldn't understand what motives she had. Maybe she knew I was in love with her and just wanted me out of her life. I was tempted to find Katherine and tell her the truth but knew that at this point, it was Lily's word against mine, so I would only embarrass myself. I was so disgusted at the situation that the idea of waiting till eleven to leave was becoming the real torture. I felt I had nothing more to do here and time slowed to a painful pace. When I did go down, at eleven on the dot, the lobby was empty. I had to sit on one of the chairs lining the walls for what felt like an eternity. Katherine eventually came in, gave me the bag and wished me good luck. She said she had faith I would find a new home, she also asked me never to contact Lily, saying it was best to leave the past where it belonged. She then pointed me toward a taxi she had called, which was to bring me to the closest train station.

We drove down the beautiful drive, lined with beautiful maple trees, offering their vulnerable naked bodies to the wet winter wind. When we cleared the large gates, I had a feeling I was leaving what had been a fairytale, to return to the real world of suffering. I felt a deep sense of rejection, too powerful to be inflicted by another human, it was as if fate itself wanted me to surfer; alone. I could now see Sysiphus, admiring the huge rock he had painfully pushed to the top of the hill, only to realise it was in fact moving, steadily rolling down at first, then gradually picking up speed, destroying anything that lay in its path.

While he watched it, powerlessly, he remembered this had happened many times before and knew fate would impose this on him yet again. The thought didn't make him stop though, his body just got back into gear, walking down the hill after his rock, driven by something greater than logic, a sense that "shit happens" and that when you're at the bottom, things can only go one - upwards.

Chapter Six

Finding love in Paris

It was mid-May and I had just graduated from the University of Bath, with a degree in Politics - I felt good it was over although I had no idea what to do next. A lot of my friends like Lottie had decided to go on to do a master's degree. For my part, the apparition and subsequent disappearance of Nicolas had shaken my world. Even six months later, I would stay up at night, lying in my bed, thinking about him. I remembered him for his warm smile, and his darting green eyes; animated by his vivid intelligence. A vision of the night I went to his room would soon germ in my mind, the way he had taken care of me, the way he acted in such a sensitive and protective way. He was both a strong and kind man. My imagination would then come up with various scenarios, usually involving me asking him to join me in his bed - I deeply regretted not having done so; then we would kiss, wrap our bodies against each other, I would feel his warmth, and gradually get wet, slowly touching myself as I imagined his long erect penis press against my waist - it would draw me even closer until there was no space left to separate us.

These fantasies weren't the healthiest things to do, and I knew it, as once these dreams would come to an end, they would leave me feeling empty. I still didn't understand why he left in such a hurry and this led my mind to repeatedly revisit the question. I knew something must have happened, I was still convinced he wasn't the type to run away without saying goodbye. I had all sorts of theories as to why he did. I initially thought he disagreed with our way of handling the issue and wanted to find someone else to help him divulge the secret he carried, but that didn't explain why he left in such a rush. I even tried asking my father whether they had a falling out over something but it didn't seem to be the case. My father even seemed as surprised as I was that Nick had evaporated like the morning dew. Somehow I found it hard to trust him, and this hurt me, I had always been close to my Dad. This pain stopped me from asking him further questions and gradually, a trench of spite was excavated, each aching spade driving us further apart. These thoughts were driving me away from the things I loved, I struggled to spend much time at Lymington Hall; the rooms would carry the memories of Nicolas, the corridors the echos of his betrayal.

It sometimes felt very surreal, I mean, he had just entered and left my life in such a fast and brutal way that it felt like I had just dreamt it all. I had been scared for my mental health until the intense revision before my final exams had saved me, occupying my mind enough to keep me sane, yet the salvation of this temporary distraction had now come to an end and my mind was on its way back to its fruitless ruminations.

I had decided to travel a bit as I didn't know what I wanted to do in life. Deep down I did know I just wanted to be with Nicolas.

I never told anyone about the conversations we had at Lymington Hall during that week of November. It was as if the memory of Nicolas had taken over all the space in my mind, so even information of such a magnitude - such as the end of the world - was buried so deep in my mind it had little chance to surface. I guess that in some ways I was also trying to protect myself from the truth. This didn't stop me from knowing that my life was to be a short one, so I wanted to experience it to the fullest; there was little point in doing a masters in this context, or some badly paid internship to gather work experience; so travelling felt like the best solution.

I kept speculating on what Nicolas had become. He left without a passport, so he must still have been somewhere in the country. He knew I went to the University at Bath, so a part of me lived in the hope that he would come to find me, safe to say he never did, and now he never would as I was leaving for good.

We had had a long week of celebrations after handing in our dissertation, it was the end of May by the time we set off to London feeling tired but excited. We were going to Paris. It had been a while since I had last been on the Eurostar and I couldn't help but admire what a feat of engineering it was; while also thinking these tunnels might become very popular in the next nine years. I could imagine millions of people walking, sitting and lying in the tunnels, all the way to Paris. It was an odd feeling for me to be the only one to know the world was about to end. In a way it made everything more vivid, it made life feel more fragile. I felt so grateful for each ray of sun that stroked my face, so emotional when watching the sunset over the

Somerset hills. The knowledge that everything and everyone around me was soon to disappear made it all the more desirable. I did, however, suffer from the fact no one around me knew, it made me feel detached from my friends, deep down I wanted to share this secret with them but felt incapable of explaining it all. Was it the fear of them thinking I had gone mad? - like I did when Nicolas first told me - Or was it because I wanted to protect them? I think it was because they all seemed to be happy in their lives, I didn't feel it was my place to disturb them.

As we got off the Eurostar at about half past two in the afternoon, we walked to our friend's flat which was situated at the top of the Rue des Martyrs, just below Montmartre. It was only a fifteen-minute walk and we didn't have many bags, so we walked from Gare du Nord, across the large boulevards with their tables pouring onto the streets, loaded with beautifully dressed people enjoying a late lunch in the spring sun. Arriving in Paris was such a pleasure to my senses, the smells lingering around restaurants and bakeries, the light filtering through the large maple trees lining the large boulevards, the dark green of the benches with their couples on them, shamelessly eating each other's faces off, as their passion overpowered the social construct of pudity.

We spent the most wonderful week, visiting so many museums and galleries that my legs couldn't keep up with the sheer distances between the infinity of beautiful art the city had to offer. The city was alive with a love for the good things in life. Men looked sexy with their dark curly hair emerging from their unbuttoned shirts, and women walked with such confidence in their loose-fitted dresses, leaving the fabric to dance in the music of the spring wind. We would then go out at night, to a multitude of different bars, chatting away with random people, it was clear the Parisian boys liked the look of us and had no shame in showing it. I found them very attractive, especially the way they spoke about their emotions, showing so much more sensitivity than most boys I had been with in England. They seemed fearless at the idea of making themselves look vulnerable while also being so masculine - what an exciting combination! - It felt deeply refreshing and was a great way to have meaningful discussions.

That Friday night, we all got ready to go to a party at a large house on the Isle of Saint Louis. I was wearing a yellow linen cocktail dress which I had managed to buy in some vintage shop two days earlier. I was obsessed with it - I have to say it was rather short - but it gave me the look of one of those iconic 70's air hostesses and made me feel very sexy. Although I wore it to feel good about myself, the stares picked up on the pavements were a confirmation of my desirability, and that's what I liked about it - there was a part of me that also knew I wanted something more than a stare. Girls don't wear lipstick for their boyfriends who are as a result unable to kiss them, they do it to show the world they are still worth being desired. With this in the back of my mind, we had met a group of friends at a bar before going, and that's when I first met Dimitri Yousoupov.

He was a fascinating individual, half French, half Russian, speaking perfect English - he went to boarding school in England from an early age - he had a vivid imagination and was very well mannered; as well as having an allure of naughtiness about him that I found very seductive. He also looked like the spitting image of Nicolas, although his personality was very different, he had more assurance about him, even arrogance - features that Nicolas kept for himself. Dimitri had beautiful grey eyes, and a powerful athletic build combined with an elegant, determined-looking face. They did of course have their differences, firstly Dimitri didn't share the same beautiful green eyes as Nicolas, and they weren't animated by his incessant thirst for understanding, secondly, Dimitri's hair was long and thick, which further softened his features, giving him the aura of prince charming, rather than the more rugged look Nicolas had. I couldn't keep comparing the two of them in my mind.

We hit it off straight away, talking about the best way to die after just a few minutes of meeting each other. He told me he was a Stoic at heart, loving the idea of the death of Socrates, drinking the Hemlock poison surrounded by his loved ones, dying for his philosophical convictions, and accepting the ruling of the Athenian democracy despite him disagreeing with it. I found this all quite melodramatic and cliche, so I teased him in a flirtatious way, challenging him by saying I didn't believe he was a man who would welcome death in such a way. I was teasing him, but I also knew it to be true, he was too arrogant to die like Socrates, but I left that part out. Again this conversation had brought me back to the debates we had had at Lymington Hall, when the thought crossed my mind, a sense of nostalgia enveloped me, it took me away from the present, snatching me away from my bistrot chair, stealing me away from this beautiful Parisian terrace and taking me to a place where you could visit memories - but only for a second - before being sent back to the reality that I was staring vacantly into Dimitri's eyes.

He held my stare and asked: "Is everything okay Lily?" to which I answered "Yes, what you said reminded me of a lovely memory", he looked at me and laughed; "you mean the death of Socrates reminded you of a lovely memory?". We both laughed at this, raising our glasses and smiling forcefully at each other.

After a few drinks at that bar, we decided to walk to the party, meandering through the streets that lead to the Isle Saint Louis was so beautiful. I had had a lot of wine at this point, I think it was because there was something wrong about flirting with Dimitri, there was a part of me trying to imagine it was Nicolas, and hopping a few more glasses of wine would blur the difference. Dimitri and I walked together as we left, distancing ourselves from the rest of the group. He made me laugh a lot, I was in the best mood, I felt so full of life, as if I was breathing for the first time in a while. It felt very special, like I had a new blood type flowing through my veins. It felt sweeter, less dry, with more body, more complexity, like a well-aged Bordeaux - my body was devouring it; I felt that each inch of my body was feasting on life.

Dimitri took me by the hand, telling me he wanted to show me a beautiful art-deco building which was in a side street - he must have guessed I was obsessed with architecture because I hadn't ever told him. "We'll catch them up in a sec," he said pointing to the others ahead. There was no building, or at least we never got to it. As soon as we were out of sight, he put both his warm hands on either side of my cheeks, looked straight into my eyes, and said: "You're so beautiful" and kissed me. Not the most original pickup line but he was hot and I was horny. What started as a delicate kiss from him, quickly turned into a frenzy. I grabbed his face, pressing my lips hard against his, pushing my tongue deep into his mouth, biting his lower lip, pressing my body against his to feel his erect penis against mine. I felt sweat pouring out of my glands, my throat grew dry - I could feel myself getting wet and puffy down there. I took his hand, directing it slowly down, and into my panties, before slipping his flies open, sliding my hand inside his, and grabbing his erect penis. It was so hard, so long, so warm and smooth. We both groaned in pleasure, losing ourselves in the moment, transported by pleasure. The frequency of his moans became faster, they got louder, and seconds later I felt a warm jet against my hand. He rested against the wall, looking at me with a mixture of surprise, gratitude and embarrassment. He said in a slightly childish tone; "I don't usually cum so fast". Rather than answer, for some reason I took my hand which was covered in his sperm, and put it in my mouth, after which I kissed him, returning to the seamen to their boat. I think he was a little shocked but seemed to love it. Men love to be surprised when having sex - however disturbing the surprise is. We caught up with the group, without saying a word about what happened and got to the party. Safe to say that we didn't spend much time there, after twenty minutes, we went straight back to his flat, tore each other's clothes off - like overexcited children attacking the wrapping on their Christmas presents - and fornicated in a frenzy, like two wild beasts, in a desperate hurry to share each other's fluids, trying our best to interlock the angularities of our bodies into united shape.

As the lights filtered through the curtains, I lay in bed looking at him, realising the craziness of last night. A feeling of embarrassment took hold of me, I told myself I was a woman and that there was no reason why I shouldn't take pleasure in men, yet I knew the guilt came from the knowledge that although he was similar, he was not Nicolas. I knew this was wrong, even pretty messed up - the idea of having sex with a clone, or a doll to satisfy my longing for him. There was also a part of me that thought I could have made it a little harder for Dimitri, rather than pouncing on his penis. I felt ashamed and dirty about the things I had done that night, the thought of some of it made my whole body cringe. What had I been thinking? I slipped out of bed and into the shower, hoping to cleanse my soul in some way. Dimitri dropped me back home at the top of the Rue des Martyrs on the back of his loud motorbike, it was a black Ducatti that made your entire body shake as soon as it accelerated. He took my number and pleaded with me to let him know my next availability for a date. My phone had run out of battery, so I told him I would message him once I had access to my calendar, which of course I knew was empty. I kissed him on the cheek and went up the circular staircase to our flat.

I told Lotties about it - without leaving any details out, we laughed, she had also hooked up with one of the guys at the party, and we exchanged quite graphic details, I was happy not to be the only one to have given myself away - although it still left me feeling a little cheap. We concluded it was what Paris did to young girls like us. Feeling a little better about myself, as the city was now to blame for turning me into a lioness on heat; we set off to go down to Le Marais to visit some galleries, and that's when it all happened.

Chapter Seven

Man Made From Clay

I walked into a random gallery with Lottie, picking the pamphlet to read a little about the art on display. The artist's name was Nicolas Popov. I froze, could it be Nicolas? But how? It was the same surname but it was impossible - just six months ago he had been at Lymington Hall, and he never mentioned anything about being artistic. How could he suddenly be an upcoming artist? I realised Nicolas Popov was probably a fairly common Russian name, so relaxed and read on - there was no way it was the same person. The pamphlet talked about the artist's desire to highlight the absurdity of our modern society, the way humans had diverged from their animalistic origins to a point of losing consciousness of what made life worth living. It talked about the fracture between our biological self and our digital world, the dissociation between the objective matter we were made of and the intersubjective world humans believed in. I walked around the space, inspecting the Artist's work. They were earthy-looking heaps of clay, looking both fragile and powerful at the same time, as if they had been made from lava, crackling as they cooled after a violent volcanic eruption. I mentioned the coincidence of the name to Lottie, who agreed there was no way it could be Nicolas. The last time she had seen him was the day we found him in the greenhouse at Lymington Hall, in his damp military uniform, stumbling out in an explosion of flower pots. We had never talked about him since. Although we agreed it wasn't him, I couldn't help but see something in the artist's work that was a part of him. The fragility, the heat of the oven that solidified the clay, the search for meaning. I brushed this idea aside, remembering I had just had sex with Dimtri because I saw Nicolas in him.

I went up to the reception desk and asked when the Artist was next around, even if it was evidently not him - a part of me wanted to be sure. She looked up at me, with a judgemental look, quite typical of French gallery employees, and asked why I wanted to see him.

I blurted out the first thing that crossed my mind: "I'm a journalist, and I would like to ask him a few questions about his work".

She looked at me with a sceptical look and answered: "Well di artist das not like de journaliste, but eehh...we have a press conferance here tomorrow, at five, so you can dry, but don't hope too much Madam".

I thanked her and left. I then thought I might as well ask what he looked like before coming all the way back tomorrow, but then decided that would sound a little weird so I tried to google him, hoping a photo would come up. There were loads of pictures, all of different men called Nicolas Popov, some had just graduated from an American university or proudly holding large fish in their hands, others sailing or swimming with sharks, but none doing sculpture, so the search led to nothing. We went to a few more galleries and then out to dinner. I was lost in thought, Lottie could tell so and she tried to ask me about it, I usually tell her everything but I couldn't quite talk about Nicolas, in any case, I had decided to turn up the next day.

I don't know why I couldn't talk to my best friend about him, I just felt my love for him was a secret I couldn't give away - it was also embarrassing as it gave away an obsessive trait of my personality. I guess I was also trying hard to deny the existence of that love, which had been obsessing me ever since he left, I knew that the more I talked about it, the stronger the feeling would become. It had already ballooned into a delusion, a crazy infatuation for him, a platonic love which I knew no one could understand; each thought would feed this monster - it would keep growing, spreading like a disease, infecting my soul. It was all crazy - we had never kissed, yet I felt he already owned a part of my soul. I was fully aware of how mad this sounded so decided to keep it to myself. So I decided to tell Lottie I thought it would be funny to pretend to be journalists and turn up to the press conference. She knew me well enough to understand this was more than a game but she didn't ask any questions.

The next day, I walked into the gallery with determination, my heart pumping, trying my best to control my breathing. I looked around and saw the Artist immediately. He was hard to miss as he was surrounded by a flock of journalists, some clutching microphones, others notebooks, all facing the short, fat, bald man who was the sculptor. The plump man was waving his hands at the sculptures while answering questions - confidently shedding light on his artistic genius with great pride. Although I had done my best to convince myself it was never going to be Nicolas, seeing this short old man destroyed me. I could feel my legs giving way below me and nearly fell to my knees. All my hopes shattered in a single glance. It was as if I had spent the last six months carefully crafting this beautiful crystal vase, symbolic of my love for Nicolas, and this fat little man had sent it crashing, in a million sharp glittering shards of ice. I walked straight out, followed by a puzzled Lottie. When I arrived outside, I started gasping for air, my throat was constricted and I was having a bit of a panic attack. Lottie looked with a worried expression and asked "Are you okay? I had no idea this press conference meant so much to you? Is it about Nicolas? I thought you just helped him out that day in the greenhouse and then never saw him again".

She took me in her arms: "I had no idea you loved him like this" she said.

I pushed her away, feeling so stupid. I couldn't believe I had gone to this ridiculous press conference, I couldn't believe I was acting in such a pathetic way, how could I believe I was going to find him here? In a gallery in Paris? Had I gone Mad? I felt so weak, so stupid.

When my breathing returned to normal I said to her: "No I don't love him, for that matter I hate him, he just came into my life, and ruined it. I was happy, I was content with my life. He just came and took over my mind, spreading like cancer, I hate him, I want this to end!"

I tried hard to stop the tears of frustration that were building up, ready to flood down my cheeks, I felt all the strength leaving my body to the point I had to sit on a chair from a neighbouring terrace.

Lottie sat next to me and said: "So did you see him after that day we first met him? Did anything happen between the two of you".

I tried my best to calm myself down and not ask her to stop asking questions. I looked down, I was so angry at myself, my eyes were about to burst, I couldn't even quite make eye contact with her. I thought to myself *'what the hell, I might as well tell her how much of an idiot I am'*, so pronounced in a loud, frustrated voice: "Yes, he spent a couple of weeks at Lymington Hall. Nothing ever happened, he just got to me, it's as if a Russian charlatan cast a spell on my soul you know? I'm now scared of him, I was so happy in life when I met him, I was just a student doing my best, life was easy and then, he just destroyed it all. He's like the snake that persuaded Adam and Eve to eat the apple. He brought so much pain by making me see the evil truth, I need to get rid of his memory, I need to get him out of my head, it's driving me mad, it's driving me bonkers!" Lottie hugged me and I added: "I hate the way he's caused me so much pain!". Her arms told me to calm down, her warmth made me feel grateful to have a friend that understood me. I was lost in her embrace until I heard a familiar voice. A very familiar soft Russian accent.

"I'm so sorry to have caused you such pain Lily, it was never my intention." I swung round and looked at him, stunned by his sudden apparition. It was him. I stared at him, my brain couldn't quite process his sudden apparition. I couldn't say a word, I just stared at him looking terrified. He looked back at me, his eyes were suddenly filled with deep melancholy, he was shaking his head gently as he added "I was never quite able to believe you were the one to ask me to leave Lymington Hall, but now I see it's true. I guess this gives me the closure I needed. I thank fate for sending you here to deliver the answer I longed for. I wish you the best of luck in forgetting me... Oh, and enjoy the time you have left". The last sentence was pronounced in an icy tone. He turned around and left, without saying goodbye. I sat there, staring at him, stunned. Then I stood up and ran towards him as if possessed by a foreign force, crying his name across the street. He turned around when I was about ten metres away from him and shouted with the most tremendous force in his voice "Leave me alone!". I froze as if the sound waves had hit me in the face, and watched as he walked away. I felt the passersby's eyes fall upon me. The French were delighted to see such a melodramatic scene of tragic love. I stood there, in the middle of the street, so baffled by what had just happened that I didn't even feel like crying. I had managed to find the man I had loved like no one else on this planet and pushed him away, my brain just couldn't process it. I just stood there, not caring about the fact everyone was staring at me. I just watched him get smaller and vanish at the end of the street. He was gone, again. I laughed like a madwoman, shaking my head again and again, I laughed at how fate was so skilful at the use of irony to torture me.

Chapter Eight

Le dessert

As I turned the corner of the street, I stopped, leaning my back against the wall. I was possessed with rage, I felt I just wanted to break something, punch someone. My teeth were clenched, and I was gripping my jacket in my left hand with all my strength, to the point that my hand had gone numb and white. I just couldn't believe what had just happened. How was this possible? Why the hell was Lily at my first press conference? I knew I needed to go back, Francois would go mad when he found out I just stormed off but I couldn't go back, I couldn't face the idea of seeing her again. What had I done for her to hate me so much? I walked on and then broke into a run, deciding to go straight back to the studio. I would have to face up to Francois later. I got to my studio which was the basement of a small block of flats just off the Place des Vosges. It was an amazing place Francois had managed to provide for me. I was so grateful to him each time I walked through the large wooden door, down the vaulted hallway, along the courtyard and into my studio. When I eventually got inside I breathed, this was my little island of peace. I decided to channel this confusing energy into a new work of art. I put some Schoenberg on the speakers, full volume, in an attempt to block out the noise of my thoughts, went up to the storage room, took a fresh block of clay, and tore the plastic wrapping off - as if hungry to get my sustenance through a new creation - and got to work. As soon as I started punching the clay to flatten it, I knew what I was going to make. I rarely ever know what I'm going to make until I have made physical contact with the clay, it then becomes crystal clear, in the form of a feeling - and my hands bring it to life. I was so immersed in my work that I only just noticed my phone had been going off, its ringtone drowned by the dramatic melodies of Schoenberg. I saw five missed calls from Francois. I sent him a quick text saying I was feeling very inspired, and was back in the studio and added I was going to switch off my phone. After I did so and chucked the lifeless phone on the bed, pushing away the thought of Francois having to face the journalists alone. I set all this guilt aside and pressed on with my work, tearing at the clay, allowing my rage to mould the block of mud. I worked very fast, in a kind of hypotonic state that allowed no room for my mind to interfere. After a couple of hours, I finished it and put it in the oven.

I had made a large lily, which I painted with an ivory-white shiny patina, with a slight green tone to it on the edges. I had planted a pile of horse dung in the middle of it, which I painted in a dark brown patina. I put it in the oven, smoked a cigarette and went to lie on the bed, on the small mattress I had set in the corner. It was where I slept when I was too exhausted to get back to my flat in République. I lay in my bed, sweating. It was getting warmer at this time of year and when the oven was on, the temperature in the room was pretty unbearable despite all the large windows being open. The events of the day caught up with me, suddenly flooding my mind. I didn't want to think about Lily, yet it was impossible not to. I decided to switch my phone on to distract myself, while the sculpture finished cooking.

Unsurprisingly, Francois had sent me a message saying he couldn't believe I had done this to him. I felt awful, so embarrassed for letting him down. He had been so good to me, treating me like a son, and nurturing my artistic talent without expecting anything in return. I knew he did it because he believed in me and felt horrible proving him wrong by letting him down. I decided to call him: He answered "Hallo, Francois a l'appareil "

I said: "Francois, I'm so sorry".

The other line went blank for a moment before he answered: "I do nat no what it is dat I can do for you Nicola"

I told him I was very inspired, and maybe a little scared of the journalists, to which he said: "Stop talking Merde, Nicola, I know you, you are scared of notting".

He was half right, I wasn't scared of journalists but little did he know, I was terrified at the idea of seeing Lily. He told me he wanted to see me at the gallery early the next morning. I told him about the piece I did, describing it as a water lily with a large poo placed on it, adding that I had decided to call it "Le Dessert".

He asked me why, so I told him that today felt like the end of a large meal, which had consisted of eating shit. I could tell by his tone that he was utterly unconvinced, but it cheered him up a little and he asked me to bring it with me the next morning.

I decided to go off into the night with the sole aim of getting very drunk. I had some friends I could have called, but didn't really want anyone to see me in this state and certainly didn't want to talk to anyone. I just wanted to chase all these confusing thoughts out of my mind and fall into a deep sleep. I went to the closest bar and ordered a double Whiskey, which annoyingly reminded me of the nights at Lymington Hall, so I downed the glass and switched to my native Vodka; I had never really liked the drink, it tasted like nothing when served as it should be, as cold as ice - but that was the point of it really - it was a painkiller, designed for that effect, not for taste. I kept on looking at the door, worried that Lily would enter this small forgotten bar in a side street of Le Marais, she was somewhere in this city, and the thought drove me crazy. I eventually went back home, not having achieved the drunkness required to drown the pain; but I was too preoccupied to keep drinking due to tomorrow's meeting with Francois.

I woke up early that morning with a bad headache, I wasn't used to drinking and it didn't agree with me. I had some time so decided to pass by my flat in Republique to take a shower and change clothes. I was feeling anxious about my meeting with Francois and felt there was no need to make matters worse by smelling of booze and sweat. I Passed by the studio on the way to the gallery - to pick up my latest sculpture - and arrived at the Gallery with a large ball of bubble wrap in my arms. I took a breath and walked through the glass door; I had arrived half an hour before I had been expected to show up. Francois Pampon was already there, he was a legend in the Parisian art world. He was a short fat man, with a gentle belly that showed a healthy love for life. He would always wear a different-coloured pair of thick-framed circular glasses, which only added to his bubbly personality. It was hard for him to pronounce a sentence without swearing, he would criticise and complain about everything, but never in a malicious way. It was just his way of being perfectly French. He was a good person and had helped me when I most needed it, hence why I felt so horrible about letting him down at the worst moment. I was dreading this conversation and walked up to him feeling like a child who's just returned after running away from home; feeling stupid about his impulsive need for freedom. I pursed my lips, I had decided to tell him the full truth. I told him I appreciated what he had done for me more than anything, that he was right that I didn't fear facing journalists, but this girl had been there, a weird story from the past. I told him I overheard her saying some very disturbing things about me, which put me in a rage and I had to run off, feeling I needed to channel that rage into this new work, pointing at the bubble wrap. I did my best to explain how this anger opened a door deep within me, and I knew I needed to exploit this inspiration while it was fresh, so I ran back to the studio and got to work. He said nothing to this but he seemed reassured to hear the truth. He pointed at my ball of bubble wrap and said: "Alors, voyons le résultat de ta douleur". I unravelled it, constantly glancing at him, trying to discern whether he liked what he saw. His approval meant the world to me. Once it was fully unravelled, we both looked at it for a moment. I looked at him again, his fist was against his chin, like Rodin's thinker. His face was expressionless; I knew he was processing my art, taking it in fully. Then, slowly, I saw a smile draw itself and illuminate his face, he continued to look at it and started nodding. He then turned towards me and said - "Bravo Nicolas, tu ne césseras de m'impressioner!" - and gave me a hearty pat on the back. I didn't quite understand what he meant but knew we had made peace.

He told me that I would have to visit all the journalists individually now that I had missed the conference. I knew this was going to require a lot more time but agreed to it without a second thought, thanking him again for his efforts and guidance. We went off for a nice lunch and a drink and he gave me a letter. He explained that a young British girl in great distress, who he assumed was the one that had driven me away, had dropped it off late yesterday evening. He gave me a little smile saying he didn't understand how a man could run away from such a woman. I gave him a bit more context about her, and I told him about the way I met her. He knew my story and was quite fascinated to hear some more about how I arrived in England. He smoked a lot and nearly choked with laughter at the idea of me in a footman's uniform working for British aristocrats. I was very happy to talk to someone about it, Francois was also the type that had heard and lived the craziest stories, so there was little judgement left in him. We exchanged a hug and a few pats on the back - as was to be expected when saying goodbye to Francois - and I went off down the road, shoving the letter in the pocket of my black baggy linen trousers. I did so with a gesture of nonchalance as if it was just some unimportant piece of paper; I was just trying to prove to myself I didn't care. This was clearly all but true as I spent the whole walk not being able to think about anything else, I kept on putting my hand in my pocket, just to feel it. I even nearly walked straight into a lamp post while I was having a quick peep at it, to see what kind of paper the envelope was made of.

Realising how stupid I was being about this, I eventually decided to read it, so I sat on one of the green Parisian benches, in a small park at the corner of the Rue Payenne.

I took in the surroundings, there was a pond with three statues of the virtues in the middle of it. Some children were running around the stone borders of the fountain with their miniature cars, vibrating their young lips to imitate the sound of loud motor engines. Pigeons were flocking around an old woman who was feeding them. It was in the middle of Paris, yet other than the sound of children playing, pigeon cooing and water cascading, it was blissfully quiet. I took the letter out to inspect it. It had *Nicolas* written in large letters on the front, my heart started to beat faster as I recognised the untidy handwriting of the literate Lily. I opened with care and started to read:

Dear Nicolas,

Yesterday came as the greatest shock. I'm so sorry to have hurt your feelings, I promise it was the last thing I would have wanted to do. I'm writing in the hope that you will find a place in your heart to see me. All I want is to have the opportunity to explain my hurtful words. To be honest, my mind is a mess and you're the only person that can help me right now.
Please message me on the number below and let's go for a coffee. Please accord me this last favour. I need this.

+447399882882

Yours,

Lily

I re-read these words a couple of times, trying to take them in. She had clearly written the letter in a rush. I put the letter back in its envelope and walked off. Her tone was not as I remembered it, she had never been so pleading. She seemed very distressed and this thought - despite the anger I had felt against her - really hurt me. I went back to the studio to try and work but no inspiration came to me. I had a meeting early the next morning with *Le Figaro Magazine* so I decided to go back home and make myself some dinner before getting to bed early - I hadn't slept so well the night before and needed some rest. After having had some dinner and watching a documentary about the power of mushrooms, I tried to close my eyes. Despite feeling very tired, the only thing I could think about was Lily and the distressed tone of her letter. The thought of her suffering kept me up, I felt this urge to protect her. As I was unable to sleep, I decided I might as well send her a message. After fetching the letter which I had left on the kitchen table, I saved her number on my phone and sent her a Whatsapp; saying bluntly that I agreed to meet her for lunch.

I walked out of the Figaro offices at noon feeling pretty good about myself - it was my first proper interview and I knew it had gone well - it felt surreal to think I had been in Siberia just six months ago and was now being interviewed by a major French magazine. I had also exchanged a few messages with Lily, which were all quite cold and void of any emotion; the kind you would send to a lawyer about the timing and location of a meeting. I arrived slightly early so started reading *The Second Sex*, by Simone de Beauvoir - Her arguments were original and I was desperate to catch up on good French literature. In Paris, it's sometimes difficult to keep up with the intellectual nature of conversations. Quite interestingly, it seems people's status in France was more geared towards their intellect rather than how much money or land they owned. Proving that intellect to people was a way of imposing your status in society. I didn't feel the need to do so but genuinely found this to be a much fairer and more dynamic social structure than basing everything on wealth which had been inherited.

I saw her arrive from a distance. She was staggeringly beautiful, sucking up all the energy around her, both the men and women she crossed could not help but look at her - she would have made the world's worst spy. She was wearing a beautiful yellow dress which made her long legs look very elegant. Her walk was also very confident - her strides seemed to be punching through the air, and her heels rang against the pavement - announcing her imminent arrival.

She was wearing large black sunglasses that concealed her expression which made me uneasy as I was yearning to read her expression. The purposefulness and pace of her step made me think she hadn't seen me and was going to walk straight past me, but when she was only a couple of metres away, she slowed down, waved with a smile and sat next to me before I could even stand up to say hello. She took her sunglasses off to kiss me hello on both cheeks, as Parisian etiquette dictates; it was evident she had been in the city for a while. As soon as her light brown almond-like eyes met mine, they seemed to be pleading for forgiveness - they disarmed me and my anger rippled away. They were so feline and quite destabilising, I did my best to compose myself.

"It's so good to see you, Nicolas," she said.

I smiled at her and replied, "It's very good to see you too".

Looking a little embarrassed, in the cutest way she said; "I'm sorry about the other day, I just really didn't expect you to be there". Seeing her made me so genuinely happy, that I didn't feel the need for any apologies. In a slightly more business-like tone, I made it clear that I had agreed to meet her because I was worried she was in a bad place. I asked what had led her to be in such a state. She looked at me for a moment, clearly trying to find the right words to describe her confused feelings. As she was about to answer, the waiter came over to take our order, slightly reliving the tenseness.

Once she had ordered her cappuccino, she looked me straight in the eyes and said: "As I told you in my letter - my mind is a bit of a mess; I don't fully understand why but I believe it's at least partly because there are some unanswered questions".

She took a deep breath and continued, "There are some questions only you can answer....so I hope to find some peace in hearing the truth directly from you".

I agreed and told her she could ask me anything she liked.

She smiled at me and said: "Thanks, I appreciate that. So, the first thing I don't understand is why you left without even saying goodbye - please just tell me the truth".

I looked at her, not believing she could have asked me such a question, but I read the sincerity in her eyes, a real yearning for the answer to her question; she even seemed desperate for my response.

I answered, quite bluntly: "Well, that's an interesting question, considering your mother told me that you were the one to ask for me to leave". Her eyebrows descended over her eyes, drawing a confused look on her face, "she said that you told her that I had behaved inappropriately when you came up to my bedroom the night you had that nightmare". As I said this her eyebrow bounced back outwards, stretching towards her hairline, with her eyes following to complete the gaping expression. I continued, with less confidence in my tone, "I have to say the fact you would lie about me in such a way hurt me, in any case, I didn't want to overstay my welcome and she told me I had to leave by eleven that same morning - I even asked her if I could stay to say goodbye to you and Bertie, but she specifically told me you had asked for me to leave while you were away". Lily's shocked expression led me to question my version of events - had she asked Katherine to kick me out of the house? Her surprised expression faded away and stillness took over her beautiful face. She stared down at her hands that were resting on the table and then cupped them around her face, her neck muscles had suddenly failed her and her head tilted towards the table, she muttered; "I can't believe her, I can't believe her, how could she?".

That's when I realised this could have been Katherine's doing, she had been so kind to me in the last days, so kind in giving me the money, the bag and the provisions that it had never crossed my mind. For the first time, Lily's perspective was starting to appear to me, like a painting in a large gallery that I was slowly walking towards. The strokes got clearer, the colours more vivid, the shapes came together and gradually I got the whole picture. She must have thought I had just left without saying goodbye while I thought she had called me a rapist. A feeling of embarrassment took hold of me, I had believed Katherine's story and never questioned it.

Lily's head was still down, and as I stared at her my remorse grew - there had been a part of me that knew Lily would never do such a thing, I was angry at myself for believing what that botoxed bitch had told me without second thoughts. I wanted to say something but couldn't quite find the words.

I eventually said "I thought it was out of character, but in my fear, it made sense that you just wanted me out of the house and made some excuse no one could question. You know Lily...despite quite a few horrible things happening to me recently, this was actually the one event that hurt me the most. I'm sorry I never questioned it, it's just I was a victim of my fate at the time, so getting rejected by you made sense in that context; it felt like it was just another blow amongst the beating life was giving me". We both just sat there, trying to process this information. She was clearly in deep shock, her hands returned to the table, and her cheeks were wet with tears but she made no noise. She didn't look up, as if unable to face my worried eyes. I put my hand onto hers, it was warm, humid and soft. Despite her apparent sorrow - a smile started to grow on my face as my brain came to terms with this information; I was starting to feel quite upbeat. It wasn't Lily, it was Katherine all along - I didn't even feel any anger towards her anymore, endorphins started to flow through my body - it was the knowledge that I wasn't hated but loved. Lily had not betrayed me, and seeing how upset she had been about this whole ordeal made me confident she even really liked me. I couldn't help but widen my smile further to include my death in this newly found joy. I took both her little hands into mine and squeezed them, she looked up at me - and with my best gleaming smile, I said: "I can't believe I got this all wrong, it makes me so happy to hear you never wanted to get rid of me". She smiled back with one of those small, vulnerable smiles. I stopped the waiter that was passing by and ordered a bottle of Rosé to celebrate, all these emotions were making me a little thirsty. As soon as the waiter nodded in assent, the mere prospect of an imminent bottle led Lily to give me a beautiful smile - a smile which drew itself over an innocent face which was still wet with the tears of sorrowful love. Her face was so pure, so beautiful, it was the face of salvation, her eyes finally understood it was all going to be okay and they thanked me. Her beauty in that moment touched me so profoundly, that my eyes started to water and my belly started to move about. I held my tears in with a smile and asked her what she was doing in Paris.

At first, she spoke sheepishly, but gradually recomposed her usual confidence - she explained that she had graduated and was with some friends, she then asked me how I got here. I told her it was quite a long story but she urged me on, telling me she had all the time in the world. I would have preferred to hear her talk about herself, but she was very insistent so I waited for the waiter to serve us some wine and got started. I told her that when I left Lymington Hall, her mother gave me four thousand pounds in cash - quite generous considering how short my footman career was. I was then dropped off by a taxi at the closest train station and took a train to London, without having given it much thought. When I got to the city, I found myself a cheap and comfortable hostel near Kings Cross and spent a couple of weeks going to galleries and museums. I had cash and thought I might as well get to know as much about the complexities of humanity and the beautiful things in life before it all ended. At the time, I was convinced Lord Mounthaven or Professor Neumann would make the information I had given them public, so my mindset at the time was very much set to living by the day. I eventually met Arvid Matta at a gallery opening in Mayfair, I explained he was a very wealthy art collector from India. We instantly made friends and he invited me to come to dinner at his house in Belgravia that same night - after a few drinks and quite the meal, we had the most amazingly open and honest conversations - we talked a lot about travelling and the luxury of having the world at our fingertips. That's when I admitted to him that I was a runaway soldier and had no passport. He took this information without judgement, begging to know more about my story. I eventually told him and the rest of the guests my entire life story, leaving out what my father told me.

Lily asked, "Why did you leave it out?".

I answered "Oh you know, people just think you're crazy when you tell them the world is going to end - as it was I had already admitted to being a Russian soldier, any more may have jeopardised my credibility. Besides, I was alone in London and needed friends at the time, so it was just easier to leave it out".

She nodded and said: "I know the feeling, sorry for interrupting, please continue".

I went on "So anyway, he told me he could get me to France. I asked how and he said he was driving there in a couple of days adding he often smuggled his dog in the back of his Porsche - just because he couldn't be bothered to fill in the papers. He told me he had never been checked. He explained that illegal immigrants want to go from Calais to Dover and not the other way round, so it did make sense, same thing for drugs and other types of smuggling, so in effect, the French border police in Dover were pretty relaxed. As you can imagine, I had only just met this guy and we had had a few drinks so I didn't expect much. He called me the next morning though, offering again, saying it would be fun and that he'd appreciate the company. It was a roll o the dice for me, if I was caught it was likely I would be sent back, but I was desperate to see the world so a few days later, we set off - and just before passing the border - I just laid down in the back with some covers on top of me with his dog. I have to say it was a piece of cake." She smiled at the very British expression I had just used. "Honestly his driving was the scariest part, but it did get us to Paris very fast. Along the route, he told me I could stay for as long as I wanted in his house in Paris, I tried to refuse politely but he insisted, so I agreed. You must think I just latch on to rich people by now" I said with a bit of an awkward smile.

She smiled and said, "No, I would say your charm makes them latch onto you". She then added quickly; "So how did you become an artist then?".

I answered "Well, Arvid had a huge studio in his house in Montmartre. The house had belonged to a sculptor who had died, leaving it in a terrible mess. He completely redid the entire place except for the actual studio, which was left in its original, poetic mess. He just felt it would be a crime to tidy it up. Arvid is pretty eccentric and claims that people's lives live through the objects they cherish, so he felt it would have been a crime equivalent to murder to clear out the studio. One evening, after a drinks party, we came back with four of his friends and decided to go to the studio and just do some art. None of us were artists but we felt inspired and decided it could be fun. We mixed some plaster, adding to the fantastic mess, and that's when I did my first sculpture. I have to say it was the weirdest feeling for me. As you know the last few years have been pretty intense for me, there's a lot of noise in my head, these voices keep arguing in my mind, and a part of me believes I should be telling people the truth about what is going to happen to them, the other part tells me I should just try to protect myself. I also have this constant feeling that my parents are judging my actions from above - anyway, as soon as I had the plaster in my hands - I relaxed and everything went quiet. It was the craziest feeling. I don't really know how to describe it, but it's as if you are suddenly propulsed into the middle of a huge dark room, with a spotlight on you. There is nothing around, it's just you and the clay. Arvid was also very encouraging - I'm really not so sure I'm even much good as an artist but he has been pushing me to become one. In any case, from that night onwards - I got completely addicted to it. I ended up spending about fourteen to sixteen hours a day in the studio over about two weeks. I felt a bit embarrassed about it, I even told Arvid that I couldn't continue being his benefactor - I just felt too guilty about not doing any tangible work. At first, he told me I had brought the old sculptor back to life by using his tools and studio; when I insisted I needed to go he got quite annoyed at me and explained to me, in quite an authoritative way, that he wanted this for himself more than he wanted it for me. He told me he wanted to foster new talent and stipulated that he would be very annoyed if I didn't order new materials every morning to his secretary - adding that if I failed to do this, he would interpret this as a lack of gratitude on my part".

She looked at me with amusement and said: "Wow, he really does sound like a character".

I loved seeing her face get animated, I said: "Yeah, I mean he's a bit mad but in the best way. I'll introduce you to him and you'll see, deep down he's an adorable man, full of generosity, but he also has this way of making sure people do as they are told to. As for myself - I was very happy with the agreement and hated the idea of letting him down. Anyway, after about two weeks, he brought Francois to the studio. I work very fast and I was in full discovery mode, so I had literally filled every millimetre of space with sculptures by then".

She looked at me, her eyes glowing, I could tell she was thoroughly enjoying this story. "Who's Francois?" she asked.

I explained he was my official representative and gallerist, currently exposing my work in Le Marais. "Ah yes. Is he the one I gave the letter to?" she asked.

"Yes, that would be him, he's also been very supportive. Everyone has, including you. My bad fortune has drawn me to some wonderful people". I could tell her cheeks were going a little red at that compliment. "I mean... I fundamentally broke into your house and you gave me a job". I had been speaking for a long time and we had nearly finished the bottle of Rosé. The wine was getting to my head and I was feeling quite giddy. I had been reclining backwards on my chair as I talked to her. I suddenly had the urge to lean towards her and take her hands but was worried about her reaction - I decided to pour the rest of the wine into our glasses and suggested we go for a walk, saying I wanted to show her some of my favourite places in Paris. She seemed delighted by the idea so we finished our glasses, chatting about all sorts of different things - admiring the outfits of passers-byes and inhaling the lovely atmosphere of the Parisian boulevards. I pretended to go to the toilet and paid for the wine and coffee, when I came back and suggested we leave, she pretended to be annoyed that I paid. I have to say, considering I had been at her mercy the last time I saw her, paying was the greatest pleasure.

We walked down the boulevards, through parks, and popped into some galleries while inhaling the smell of summer. We walked aimlessly, talking about all sorts of things - from world politics to art with everything in between. It was so good to be reunited, in some ways it even felt like we had never really been separated. As the galleries started to close our meandering moved to the terraces of the many restaurants and bars that adore the long boulevard. As we drank, we got closer, glass by glass, inch by inch. At first, it was our hands that seemed thirsty to soak up each other's clamminess - eventually, our bodies yearned for more bodily fluids than our little sweaty soldiers could provide. So, as the sun set and we sat on the river bed - at the tip of the Isle St Louis, the sunset, supervised by the powerful equestrian statue of Henri IV.

That is when emboldened by the alcohol in our veins. Our faces grew closer, our hearts beat faster and our lips met, in perfect unison - two bodies became one, two halves became a whole, two drops of water combined to become one. Our kiss started off like a little flame, dancing, gently and progressively across a slightly damp piece of paper - it then started experiencing the fuel that was provided by the reciprocity of its desire, which encouraged it to grow into a roaring fire. Our tongues met, turned and twisted - Lily moaned, grasping my face with her strong fingers, pushing her lips hard against mine - lost in a frenzy of passion. I have no idea how long this lasted, but when it did eventually come to an end, we were both quiet for quite a while - both a little shocked at the violence of this passion. We eventually got back to walking, the same way as before - but for the way our bodies seemed to be terrified of any separation. We found a restaurant called *Le Polidor*, on the rue Monsieur le Prince, just next to the Theatre de L'Odeon in the Sixieme Arrondissement. It's a beautiful part of town, much quieter than Le Marais - with much fewer tourists. I was desperate to show *Le Polidor* to Lily - it was one of my favourite places in Paris. The decoration hadn't changed since the mid-nineteenth century, the waitress had worked there for over forty years, the portions were huge and the prices very reasonable. I had come to Paris not knowing anything about wine, but just like my reading of Simone de Beauvoir, I had felt the need to educate myself in order not to feel like an imposter here. *Le Polidor* had been my education in this sense, I would walk around the Jardin du Luxembourg, reading and sketching the numerous statues, until I would drop by for a couple of glasses of wine and a three-course meal. They would sit you along these long tables, in a very convivial manner that wasn't so typical in

Pairs - this led me to prefer visiting this particular establishment on my own - as I would systematically end up meeting another lost soul to share some wine and good conversation with. I ushered Lily inside, the smell of broth and the clattering of cutlery hit us with its welcoming warmth. The walls were adorned with old mirrors, oxidised by time - set in heavy art-deco wooden frames, other walls were painted in light green with an undulating floral boiserie adding some further warmth. Colette, the old waitress, recognised me immediately and found us a corner - she gave us the menu and threw me a complicit smile as if to congratulate me on the beauty of my guest and offer her help in closing the deal. We ordered based on Colette's recommendations, it was a swift process. I took Lily's hands and asked her "what do you think these places will become when people find out?". She looked at me, surprised I was bringing the subject up.

She answered: "When people find out they are going to die in nine years?". I nodded - she took a deep breath as if to show she would have preferred a more upbeat topic. "Well I guess the lovely waitress would probably stop working here, I imagine they would struggle to find a replacement, it's already hard enough as it is for restaurants to find staff. So yeah, most likely it wouldn't last long - I guess people will be more busy digging holes and trying to save their skin".

I knew she wasn't happy to discuss this topic but for some reason, I felt the need to discuss it - maybe it was the guilt that I hadn't told anyone.

I said: "I sometimes struggle at the idea of keeping this horrible truth a secret, don't you feel a little guilty about it sometimes?".

She nodded slightly and looked to her side, there were two men in their middle age, both well dressed and deep in conversation.

She said: "Yes, of course, I feel bad about keeping the truth from people, but we decided it was the right thing to do, that the truth would only create more pain".

I wasn't under the impression this had been decided, for that matter I didn't feel there had been a conclusion at all. I said: "Did you discuss it once I had left Lymington Hall?".

She stared at me for a few seconds before answering: "Well my Father brought it up a couple of times, more referring to it than actually discussing it, I know he went to visit Professor Neumann a few times, so I imagine they probably discussed it then. For my part, I was very hurt when you left, so I didn't feel like discussing it and I guess I did my best to shy away from the topic".

I pondered her last sentence, knowing this was a beautiful revelation of her feelings for me. I asked; "Did you have feelings for me before I left?".

She looked at me and smiled, leaving the pause lingering a little and enjoying the sight of my hopeful face. "Yes, I guess I did, but that really became clearer when you left". I squeezed her hands and gave her a giant smile - At that moment I wished the table wasn't separating us, it felt like a football pitch, cruelly stopping me from kissing her.

I asked: "So what's the plan? How long are you planning on staying in Paris for?".

She looked a little disappointed at my question and just answered: "There is no plan, do you have a plan?".

I answered that I didn't have one but felt it would be smart to cash out on my art, and buy some gold - as I believed that the news was going to come out sooner or later and gold was likely to replace currency, hopefully also buy a house in the country; maybe some old farm or cottage and live the rest of my days in peace as the world around me turned to chaos. I told her I also wanted to stock up on all sorts of things, including hallucinogenic drugs, as I had done some research and wanted to try them out.

"Really?" she said, quite amused at this plan. "Why plan so far ahead, wouldn't it be better to just live in the moment a little, who knows what value your gold will have when people discover the world will end? What are the chances of your predictions about this new world being correct? No offence, but It's much more likely you will be wrong, in which case you're setting yourself up for failure".

She was right, there was no guarantee. She was so beautiful when she contradicted me, she did so in a gentle way, she would laugh - and her slender chest would vibrate. I noticed she never wore a bra, so her breasts would wobble around playfully.

I smiled and explained that gold had always been the currency people fell back on when things got nasty, this had been repeatedly proven throughout Russian history - I agreed she was right, that planning too far ahead was also setting myself up for failure, but it would be madness to ignore the information we had and not prepare for what was to come. I said: "Of course, but it reassures me to think I'm a step ahead and have things under control. Sometimes it even pushes me to ponder whether we could survive this. As Professor Neumann said, people are thinking of living on Mars right?".

She took a big sip of wine and said: "What is the point of living in a tunnel? I prefer to die alongside the people I love rather than be the one to see them all die. Sometimes I feel that mortality is what makes life so precious, it's a gift to die before or with your loved ones. My grandmother died when she was just over a hundred, she saw all her friends, siblings and even one of her sons die before her. I'm not sure I would choose to live that long over dying at an early age". There was a part of me that agreed that dying past one hundred was a little much. I thought to myself that at least I would certainly not be living into my old age, what troubled me more than anything was the fact I didn't have much control over the way I was going to die. It was like this big unknown, constantly looming over me.

On the one hand, I had the certainty that my life was soon to come to an end yet, on the other, I didn't quite know how. Would there be a lot of pain? Would it be epic or pathetic? I also had this weird unexplainable feeling that the end was going to be red. Maybe it was because Professor Neumann compared our planet after the tragedy to becoming similar to Mars - but I was sure it was something else. Something deep within me, it was an instinct I could feel without quite being able to understand it. Something that I had never learnt was telling me that this Red was the power of evil and that, in nine years, it would take over.

I decided to tell Lily about this, she was pretty surprised but was open-minded enough to listen to me fully. She said; "You know, I think we have been fed this idea that red is bad and white is good. You know, from the colour of blood, or fire and all that".

"It's funny you said that, I also see white as good, but this feeling goes further - it gives me a sort of impression that I am currently white, and should join the red - you know because they are going to win in some sort of way. I don't know, it feels weird to talk about it".

She laughed and smiled at me and said; "No, I can understand it, it's probably just your subconscious which knows you're going to die and is scared. It's normal to want to save yourself, just please don't become the devil!". We laughed this abstract and absurd conversation off, she then asked me why I wanted to fill my dream house with magic mushrooms. I told her that I felt there was something written in them, as if they held some fundamental truths about nature - that you could only see when you take them.

I asked her: "Would you like to try some magic mushrooms? I have a contact that can sell me some?".

She looked at me, a little surprised and said: "I guess I could give it a try, but what is it that you like about them?".

I explained to her that although I hadn't tried them yet, I read a book on the effect of psychedelics on the brain and also watched a documentary. I asked, "Have you heard about the myth from the 1960s about the fact that the left side of our brain is the analytical, logical and verbal half while the right brain is the creative, emotional, and visual half?"

She nodded and said: "Yes, I heard about this, but as you say, I understand it's more of a myth than it is reality. Or at least what you're describing is quite a brutal simplification".

I smiled and said: "You're exactly right, but it does help to explain what psychedelics do to your brain. What we do know is that by taking magic mushrooms, you reduce your analytical and logical thinking which allows you to see the world as a whole".

She looked a little puzzled and asked: "What do you mean as a whole?"

I answered: "I mean that when you look out of the window now, you don't see the view, your eyes automatically fixate on something. For example my eyes have just fixated on that red light up there".

I pointed up at the traffic light and it turned to a vivid green almost immediately as if trying to hide away. "Yeah, I see that now," she said.

"So all that to say that, according to this book, if you are to look at a tree, rather than looking at a snippet of it, like you're looking at a snippet of the view outside, you see the entire tree".

I said this last part while waving my arms in passion, so much so that I felt I might be getting a little too excited about this topic, but she seemed to enjoy it as she smiled at me and took my hand, rolling it up into a fist and setting her two warm hands around it, like a penguin over its egg.

It felt so good to know that she loved me back, it had only been an afternoon yet I already knew it. It felt as if I had been with her for so long - at this thought, my lungs filled with air, I expired with a big smile while briefly relaxing my eyelids. When I opened them she was there, looking at me with her beautiful brown eyes, smiling delicately, enjoying the tender moment effortlessly.

We continued talking about all sorts of things, the conversation seemed to bounce around all sorts of topics in a very natural way. When we had finished our dessert, we felt as stuffed as the canard confit we had just eaten - so we decided to walk all the way back to Montmartre, which was over an hour away. We walked side by side, holding hands - occasionally stopping to share a kiss - our bodies would come together, finding cavities in the angularity of our bonny forms, interlocking to become a single mass - our lips would tenderly meet before slowly being motivated by some hidden force, quickly evolving the scene into a passionate and even carnal scene, it was as if our tongues were convinced they could grab the other person's soul in the depth of the mouth. Occasionally she would then press her hips against my erect penis with all her strength - pulling me longingly towards her with all her might - my heart would thump about at such a pace, I could feel the overloaded veins in my neck and penis scream in suffocation, it would even get painful as if I was going to lose my tail in some bloody explosion, so much so that I would eventually feel I had to put an end to this before I completely lost control of myself. We would then walk a few minutes in silence, fumbling each other's fingers. The night was warm, the light from the street lamps a mellow orange, and the smell of the river Seine was romantically nasty.

I decided I would walk her back to her flat which was on the top of the Rue des Martyrs - our legs grew heavy as we climbed up the steep hill - when we eventually got to her door, we shared a long deep kiss - full of power and impatience, as if we were trying to get our fill for the night before leaving each other - little did we know, the night was just getting started. To my great delight, she decided to invite me upstairs for tea. I accepted, trying my best to keep cool and subdue a large grin on my face, my animalistic instinct could smell there was more than tea on offer here - besides my blood was already boiling, Paris was warm, the last thing we needed was more heat.

We climbed up the twisting stairs in silence to the third floor - she warned me her housemate may already be asleep. She twisted the key in the large green door and slid it open with great care, as if she was opening the vault of a bank in the depth of the night. The tension was so high that I found myself holding my breath.

As soon as we got in she switched the lights on and said "It seems Lottie isn't back yet, shall I give you a little tour of the house?".

Instead of answering, I took her into my arms and kissed her, holding her hips tightly against mine. This time we didn't slowly go up to the carnal part, we dove straight into it - it was as if all the tension was being released into our embrace - she responded by trying to take my shirt off - struggling to get to the buttons as she frantically searched for my flesh - she quickly gave up and pulled it over my head. She then took a step back, pushing me away - panting and looking straight into the eyes. She then released into a beautiful smile, her eyes full of malice, and she turned around to show me her back. I stood there confused as to what she expected of me, a few things crossed my mind but thankfully I didn't act on them.

She helped me by saying: "Could you please help me with the zipper on my dress". I unzipped it slowly, enjoying being plunged into her intimacy - the yellow linen fabric gently slipped off her shoulders -

getting stuck around her slender hips. I stood there, admiring her elegant back as she turned around to show me the full beauty of her femininity. I breathed hard as my heart pumped fresh blood down to my penis which was now pushing against my trousers with such voracity that for a second I thought it would tear through them.

She came to me - slowly putting her hands on it and rubbing it gently. I released a deep moan as I put my hands on her soft breasts, stroking them gently and fiddling her sensitive nipples. As soon as she unbuttoned my trousers, my erect penis came swinging out like a jigsaw, celebrating its freedom. The rest happened in a blurry frenzy, we tore the remainder of each other's clothes off and made love, baptising the hallway with our love.

The feeling when I put my penis in her was like nothing I had experienced before, it was so wet, so puffy, so welcoming - it just felt so right. We went once, then moved to the bedroom and went twice then again and again till both our genitals were as raw as the morning light filtering through the curtains. We lay in bed unable to say much, words gave place to kisses. We invented a new language with the warmth of our embrace.

It felt so good, as if a new life was starting for me, the one I had dreamt about, my body felt new - the air I drew into my lungs tasted different - I was gorging myself on a new love for life. I had to run off to an interview with AD interiors, a magazine that wanted to interview me that morning. I got dressed and left her reluctantly. As soon as I walked into the street, a feeling took hold of me, as if I was a leaf blowing and dancing in the wind. So light, so full of spin, and so happy that I felt like skipping all the way to their offices.

The interview went very well, it seems they were already sold on my work and, as everyone I had spoken to - they seemed to be particularly interested in my story. It usually made me feel a little shallow to talk about it. It was the way all these journalists asked the same questions, leading me to provide the same answers over and over again - until it felt like a practised speech when it was actually my life I was talking about - full of moments of horrible pain, confusion and guilt. Today though, I felt the absolute opposite of shallow and answered their questions with passion and excitement, even going slightly over the top in the explanation behind the inspiration that led me to create certain works. Life is a comedy, but you have to play it seriously.

I walked out feeling proud and happy about the meeting. Lily had also sent me a text message saying: *"Wow! Best night of my liffffffffe!!! When are you around??XX"*. I answered by saying: *"Same here Lily! You have no idea, words can't explain how happy you make me. I need to go to the studio. Maybe meet me there later?XX"*.

I hurried to my studio to try to channel this new inspiration - I was desperate to capture the way I was feeling and in a bit of a hurry to do so, while it was as fresh as possible. When I eventually got working, I tried a few things but couldn't quite get anywhere. I wanted to play with how light I felt, the spring in my step - but unfortunately, this wasn't so compatible with the fragile clay I was using. I tried a few different types of wire but couldn't quite get onto a stimulating path.

It turns out suffering was a much greater source of inspiration to me than happiness was. Trying to illustrate emotions is also quite tricky, you need to work fast before new emotions replace the previous ones, like the impressionists racing against the changing light of the sunset -

the happiness and warmth of the setting sun was quickly disappearing to give place to the darkness of frustration, this, in turn, was starting to make me all tense, leading my fingers to lose their stroke.

This had happened a few times before, but the swing of moods had never been so violent. When Lily eventually arrived, my anxiety evaporated with the first sight of her loving smile, my muscles relaxed - weight released its grip over my shoulders. I felt light again.

I cleaned myself up and showed her around - I was very happy to give her a tour of my studio, it was an intimate part of me that I had rarely allowed anyone to see.

I was proud of how much my life had changed in the last six months - It felt good to show her that I had a new existence which wasn't dependent on her charity. We laughed about the similarities the large ceiling windows offered in comparison to those from the crystal palace we met in. We walked around the cramped space a few times while she asked quite a few questions about my sculptures; such as what my artistic process was, whether I sculpted from live subjects or my imagination and other quite banal questions that reminded me of the journalist I had met that very morning. We both gradually grew a little tired of how formal these questions felt; so ended up rolling onto the bed to make love.

We took more time to explore our bodies this time, teasing each other by making the preliminaries torturously long and, postponing the quenching of our thirst for lust till it exploded in passion. After I climaxed, I lay down beside her, with my head tucked under her armpit and my face tilted against her breast, listening and feeling her heart thump against her rib cage. As I caught my breath, I found myself observing her beautiful figure, just inches away from my eyes; that's when an idea came to my mind. Maybe if I took some magic mushrooms and looked at her naked body, it would give me the inspiration for my next great sculpture.

I slowly raised my head and asked in a shy voice, what she thought of the idea - it was a delicate question as I really didn't want her to think I was obsessed with drugs. She looked at me with an amused expression and said she loved the idea of being sculpted by me and even found the idea quite exciting - she added that she would love to take some too. Feeling relieved at how well she had reacted, I decided to send my friend a message.

Her name was Max and she came from LA - she was a pop singer and part of a few mediocre bands. I had met her in a Jazz bar one night - Max had sent me quite hungry sexual vibes that night, so much so that I told her I was gay so that she would get off my case - to which she answered: "I love to fuck gay men". I have to say I found this quite funny and took an instant liking to her, we ended up spending the rest of the evening talking about mushrooms - which is when she told me she could sell me some.

She answered my text message in a few minutes and happened to be very close - so much so that it felt like fate was handing them to us on a plate. Lily and I started to get excited and set off to meet at her house in Rue de Saintonge, a mere fifteen minutes walk away.
When Lily met Max, both instantly hit it off. I was very happy about this, especially considering Max's flirtatious behaviour the night I met her. I was also in good spirits, although they were slightly dampened by them getting into a very passionate conversation about the socio-political problems in America. I would have usually found the topic deeply interesting but at that very moment I was preoccupied with my

own thoughts - all I wanted to do was take the mushrooms and start tripping so that I could capture the wholeness of Lily's beauty. When we eventually managed to escape from her flat, we found ourselves laughing in the street about how eccentric Max was. Based on her warning that they would take quite a while to kick in, we decided to take the shrooms straight away and sat down on a bench in the nearest park. We were both a little scared, so I led the way, putting the five different shrooms into my mouth - they had a chewy and earthy texture; I did my best to make their mastication enjoyable to encourage Lily. To my great surprise, she took all five and just stuffed them into her mouth, barely bothering to even chew them. It was decided we would walk around for a bit until we felt them coming up into our system.

After walking about aimlessly in the general direction of the studio, we eventually both started to feel a slight tingling in our teeth, which according to Max was the first sign that the mushrooms were taking effect. We headed back to the studio, occasionally looking at each other's odd-looking expressions and laughing ecstatically. As she briefly stopped to look at a shop window, I took a second to admire her. She was so beautiful, it felt like I was starting to appreciate her in her full beauty for the first time, in the entirety of her elegance and beauty. Her long brown hair framed her elongated face, her slender nose set above a constant smile which always seemed animated by mischief. She was a force of life and I suddenly knew with such conviction that loving her was all I wanted to do going forward.

When we got back we went straight to taking each other's clothes off, leaving a trail of abandoned pieces of clothing leading to the bed. Sex felt different as the drug made its way through our bodies, it took more time for me to ejaculate, so we tried a few different positions. It was so exciting exploring each other's bodies with our tingling fingers. I climaxed when she was on top of me, rubbing herself against my groyne and, that's when it really kicked in - it made my orgasm last longer somehow, I felt as if I was stuck at the peak of my ejaculation, my body spasmed, twisting and turning in pleasure.

Then there was silence, as both of us processed the magnitude of the sensations we had just experienced. We just looked up at the sky through the large windows, in ore at the beauty of life - when we looked at each other, these deep thoughts were soon replaced by laughter, as both of us rolled about in bed, our bodies convulsed with hilarity.

Everything was suddenly moving as if suddenly all solids had turned to liquids, it was quite overwhelming and different to what I expected. Lying down and staring at the ceiling was also making me feel slightly nauseous, this growing discomfort convinced me it was time to get to work - so I got to my wobbly feet.

As soon as I started getting my tools together I felt better. I got my knife to start cutting out some clay - it was a large metal Ikea knife - the handle felt fresh and strong in my hand. Once everything was set on a large stool I threw a cushion on the floor and sat down on it. The workstation was set up a couple of metres from Lily, she was still lying on the bed, allowing for the best view of her body. Her flesh was so translucent, it was as if you could see through her skin and peer through the lawyers of her muscles to the depth of her soul, hidden somewhere within her bones. Her whole body seemed to be moving, as if slowly inhaling and exhaling huge breaths of air, the room was swaying, the lights vividly cascading down from the roof windows; it was as if the heavens were illuminating her sacred body, it reminded me of Michalangelo's *La Pieta*. I could feel electrons bouncing around my brain which made it hard to concentrate, each time I would stare at her for more than a second her flesh would start moving, as if it was made of a liquid trapped in some sort of bag. I was working on a way to illustrate this liquid feeling when something started to really bother me about it. I started to get quite scared that she would burst - there seemed to be a lot of pressure building behind the thick membrane of her skin. To reassure myself, I stabbed my knife into the clay model of Lily I was working on, the blade went in and came out - it reassured me as I could see that there wasn't actually a risk of the pressure bursting the sculpture, the knife just left a clean slit where the blade had entered and left.

I focused back my attention on Lily, she was looking up at the sky through the ceiling windows - a few little clouds were slowly drifting past, just by looking at them I could feel their soft texture. I stabbed the clay again, it was a wonderful feeling - there was a suction on the blade that made it so satisfying and quite hard to pull out - interestingly, the blade was harmless, it didn't destroy the sculpture at all; it just left a very slight scar that could be smudged in with the swipe of a finger. The pile of clay was small though, it would be fun to try this out on a larger body. So I stood up and walked towards Lily, sitting beside her on the bed - stroking her translucent body. I lifted the knife high and brought it down into her belly. To my horror she let out the most strident high-pitched noise - grilling my sensitive eardrums - it was not at all like the clay sculpture that hadn't reacted at all - this made no sense to me and the confusion scared me a lot, meanwhile, the screeching seemed to be freezing my brain with terror. My priority was to make the noise stop - it would give me the silence I needed to think. I pulled the knife out of her belly and stabbed again - this time to put an end to this horrible high-pitched noise; I squeezed the metal handle as the knife sank satisfyingly into her throat. Her shrieks turned to a gurgling sound, her hands curled around the knife in her throat, red liquid was spurting through her fingers. Her eyes were so full of fear, confusion and horror. This got me into a bit of a panic, I didn't want her to be scared; luckily her convulsions gradually decreased and her body returned to its tranquil recline. She was still breathing in that liquid way, a large expiration followed by large inspirations. I looked at the pile of clay and noticed it was breathing just like her. As she lay on the bed, the white sheets quickly started to turn to red - it was fascinating to observe the way the red would gain ground over the white. I observed it in ore, and a big smile came to my face when a flash in my brain illuminated me with the significance of this colour change. They were the colours I had been seeing in my dreams! They were the red and the white! It was so powerful to finally see them, I was so happy to know that my dreams were becoming a reality. The way the red colour spread, I knew it was the colour of evil slowly gaining over the pious white of the sheets, it was happening in exactly the way we had said it would. I knew, with the greatest conviction, that this red was the end of the world, the one my father had predicted. This scene of the red spreading over the white was a symbolic representation of all the volcanoes erupting together. The cosmos had provided me with a warning through these magic mushrooms; I wasn't going to be white for long; the red would submerge the white sooner or later, just like it had done with Lily. It became evident to me that the only way not to be submerged by the red was to become red. I had managed to help Lily in this transformation from white to red, she was now safe from the end of the world. If I could also transform myself and move from the white to the red, I would survive the death of our world, I would be the one to rebuild our society after it had been consumed by the red fires of hell, I would hide as a red, find Lily and build a new society with her, it would be full of love; this was now all possible, but I needed to switch camps, disguising myself in red. I took the knife and put it against my wrist which I brought up high, so that I could see the soft clouds in the background - those clouds were so soft, they reminded me of the fresh snow in Siberia.

I was going to hide under a red blanket, to join Lily and rebuild a new society with her - it felt like the most powerful decision I had ever taken; I knew it was the best decision I had ever taken. I slid the knife through my wrist, gritting my teeth as the sharp pain pinched me like the sting of a hornet - I ignored the pain and slid the blade deeper, allowing the red to flow down it. At first, it came out fast, flowing down my arm onto my shoulders; I used my other hand to spread it all over my naked body. I quickly realised that the lower my arm was the more red flowed out of it - so I camouflaged my legs in red. I lay down next to Lily, and shared my red with her - it was getting harder to move my arm, my head felt very heavy, and I suddenly felt weak - I was getting very sleepy so I let my eyes close.

I was going to sleep before being reborn in red, the colour of the new man, the colour of a new world; I smiled at this idea and a warmth took hold of me, a tidal wave of millions of arms stretched out to embrace me with their love. I followed them to the realm of darkness, a place in which there are no colours and no shadows; a place where there are no volcanoes, no lies, and no responsibilities. A place where everything is reduced to nothing, where noise becomes silence; I had entered the kingdom of peace.

Printed in Great Britain
by Amazon